MARY ELIZABE

MILLY DARRELL

AND OTHER TALES

Elibron Classics
www.elibron.com

Elibron Classics series.

© 2005 Adamant Media Corporation.

ISBN 1-4021-9093-X (paperback)
ISBN 1-4021-1805-8 (hardcover)

This Elibron Classics Replica Edition is an unabridged facsimile of the edition published by A. Asher & Co., Berlin.

Elibron and Elibron Classics are trademarks of Adamant Media Corporation. All rights reserved.

This book is an accurate reproduction of the original. Any marks, names, colophons, imprints, logos or other symbols or identifiers that appear on or in this book, except for those of Adamant Media Corporation and BookSurge, LLC, are used only for historical reference and accuracy and are not meant to designate origin or imply any sponsorship by or license from any third party.

ASHER'S COLLECTION

OF

ENGLISH AUTHORS

BRITISH AND AMERICAN.

COPYRIGHT EDITION.

VOL. 72.

**MILLY DARRELL AND OTHER TALES
BY M. E. BRADDON.**

IN ONE VOLUME.

ASHER'S EDITION

BY THE SAME AUTHOR:

ROBERT AINSLEIGH . . . . 3 Vol.
TO THE BITTER END . . . . 3 Vol.

MILLY DARRELL

AND OTHER TALES.

BY

M. E. BRADDON

AUTHOR OF "LADY AUDLEY'S SECRET," "ROBERT AINSLEIGH" ETC.

COPYRIGHT EDITION.

BERLIN
A. ASHER & CO., PUBLISHERS,

TO

DR. AND MRS. BEAMAN,

THE AUTHOR'S OLD AND VALUED FRIENDS,

𝔗𝔥𝔦𝔰 𝔅𝔬𝔬𝔨

IS AFFECTIONATELY INSCRIBED.

CONTENTS.

	PAGE
MILLY DARRELL	1
OLD RUDDERFORD HALL	179
THE SPLENDID STRANGER	235

MILLY DARRELL

CHAPTER I.

I BEGIN LIFE.

I WAS just nineteen years of age when I began my career as articled pupil with the Miss Bagshots of Albury Lodge, Fendale, Yorkshire. My father was a country curate, with a delicate wife and four children, of whom I was the eldest; and I had known from my childhood that the day must come in which I should have to get my own living in almost the only vocation open to a poor gentleman's daughter. I had been fairly educated near home, and the first opportunity that arose for placing me out in the world had been gladly seized upon by my poor father, who consented to pay the modest premium required by the Miss Bagshots, in order that I might be taught the duties of a governess, and essay my powers of tuition upon the younger pupils at Albury Lodge.

How well I remember the evening of my arrival! —a bleak dreary evening at the close of January, made still more dismal by a drizzling rain that had never ceased falling since I left my father's snug little house at Briarwood in Warwickshire. I had had to change trains three times, and to wait during a blank and miserable hour and a quarter, or so, at small obscure stations, staring hopelessly at the advertisements on the walls—advertisements of somebody's life-sustaining cocoa, and somebody else's health-restoring cod-liver oil, or trying to read the big brown-backed Bible in the cheerless little waiting-room; and trying, O so hard, not to think of home, and all the love and happiness I had left behind me. The journey had been altogether tiresome and fatiguing; but, for all that, the knowledge that I was near my destination brought me no sense of pleasure. I think I should have wished that dismal journey prolonged indefinitely, if I could thereby have escaped the beginning of my new life.

A lumbering omnibus conveyed me from the station to Albury Lodge, after depositing a grim-looking elderly lady at a house on the outskirts of the town, and a dapper-looking little man, whom I took for a commercial traveller, at an inn in the market-place.

I watched the road with a kind of idle curiosity as the vehicle lumbered along. The town had a cheerful prosperous air even on this wet winter night, and I saw that there were two fine old churches, and a large modern building which I supposed to be the townhall.

We left the town quite behind us before we came to Albury Lodge; a very large house on the highroad, a square red-brick house of the early Georgian era, shut in from the road by high walls. The great wrought-iron gates in the front had been boarded up, and Albury Lodge was now approached by a little wooden side-door opening into a stone-flagged covered passage that led to a small door at the end of the house. The omnibus-driver deposited me at this door, with all my worldly possessions, which at this period of my life consisted of two rather small boxes and a japanned dressing-case, a receptacle that contained all my most sacred treasures.

I was admitted by a rather ill-tempered-looking housemaid, with a cap of obtrusive respectability and a spotless white apron. I fancied that she looked just a little superciliously at my boxes, which I daresay would not have contained her own wardrobe.

'O, it's the governess-pupil, I suppose?' she said.

'You was expected early this afternoon, miss. Miss Bagshot and Miss Susan are gone out to tea; but I can show you where you are to sleep, if you'll please to step this way. Do you think you could carry one of your trunks, if I carry the other?'

I thought I could; so the housemaid and I lugged them all the way along the stone passage and up an uncarpeted back staircase which led from the lobby into which the door at the end of the passage opened. We went very high up, to the top story in fact, where the housemaid led me into a long bare room with ten little beds in it. I was well enough accustomed to the dreariness of a school dormitory, but somehow this room looked unusually dismal.

There was a jet of gas burning at one end of the room, near a door opening into a lavatory which was little more than a cupboard, but in which ten young ladies had to perform their daily ablutions. Here I washed my face and hands in icy-cold water, and arranged my hair as well as I could without the aid of a looking-glass, that being a luxury not provided at Albury Lodge. The servant stood watching me as I made this brief toilet, waiting to conduct me to the schoolroom. I followed her, shivering as I went, to a great empty room on the first floor. The holidays were not quite over, and none of the pupils had as yet returned. There was an almost painful neatness and bareness in place of the usual litter of books and papers, and I could not help thinking that an apartment in a workhouse would have looked quite as cheerful. Even the fire behind the high wire guard seemed to burn in a different manner from all home fires: a fact which I attributed then to some sympathetic property in the coal, but which I afterwards found to be caused by a plentiful admixture of coke; a slow sulky smoke went up from the dull mass of fuel, brightened ever so little now and then by a sickly yellow flame. One jet of gas dimly lighted this long dreary room, in which there was no human creature but myself and my guide.

'I'll bring you some supper presently, miss,' the housemaid said, and departed before I could put in a timid plea for that feminine luxury, a cup of tea.

I had not expected to find myself quite alone on this first night of my arrival, and a feeling of hopeless wretchedness came over me as I sat down at one end of a long green-baize-covered table, and rested my head upon my folded arms. Of course it was very weak and foolish, a bad beginning of my new life, but I was quite powerless to contend against that sense of utter misery. I thought of all I had left at home. I thought of what my life might have been if my father had been only a little better off: and then I burst out crying as if my heart were breaking.

Suddenly, in the midst of that foolish paroxysm, I felt a light hand upon my shoulder, and looking up, saw a face bending over me, a face full of sympathy and compassion.

O Milly Darrell, my darling, my love, how am I to describe you as you appeared before my eyes that night? How poorly can any words of mine paint you in your girlish beauty, as you looked down upon me in that dimly-lighted schoolroom with divine compassion in your dark eloquent eyes!

Just at that moment I was so miserable and so inclined to be sulky in my wretchedness, that even the vision of that bright face gave me little pleasure. I pushed away the gentle hand ungraciously, and rose hastily from my seat.

'Pray don't cry any more,' said the young lady; 'I can't bear to hear you cry like that.'

'I'm not going to cry any more,' I answered, drying my eyes in a hasty, angry way. 'It was very foolish of me to cry at all; but this place did look so cheerless and dreary, and I began to think of my father and mother, and all I had left behind me at home.'

'Of course it was only natural you should think of them. Everything does seem so bleak and dismal the first night; but you are very happy to have so many at home. I have only papa.'

'Indeed!' I said, not feeling deeply interested in her affairs.

I looked at her as she stood leaning a little against the end of the table, and playing idly with a bunch of charms and lockets hanging to her gold chain. She was very handsome, a brunette, with a small straight nose, hazel eyes, and dark-brown hair. Her mouth was the prettiest and most expressive I ever saw in my life, and gave an indescribable charm to her face. She was handsomely dressed in violet silk, with rich white lace about the throat and sleeves.

'You will find things much pleasanter when the girls come back. Of course school is always a little dreary compared with home; one is prepared for that; but I have no doubt you will contrive to be happy, and I hope we shall be very good friends. I think you must be the Miss Crofton I have heard spoken of lately?'

'Yes, my name is Crofton—Mary Crofton.'

'And mine is Emily Darrell. Milly I am always called at home, and by any one who likes me. I am a parlour-boarder, and have the run of the house, as it were. I am rather old to be at school, you see; but I am going home at the end of this year. I was brought up at home with a governess until about six months ago; but then papa took it into his head that I should be happier amongst girls of my own age, and sent me off to school. He has been travelling since that time, and so I have not been home for the Christmas holidays. I can't tell you what a disappointment that was.'

I tried to look sympathetic, and, not knowing exactly what to say, I asked whether Miss Darrell's father lived in that neighbourhood.

'O dear, no,' she answered; 'he lives nearly a hundred miles away, in a very wild part of Yorkshire, not far from the sea. But Thornleigh—that is the name of our house—is a dear old place, and I like our bleak wild country better than the loveliest spot in the world. I was born there, you see, and all my happy memories of my childhood and my mother are associated with that dear old home.'

'Is it long since you lost your mother?'

'Ten years. I loved her so dearly. There are

some subjects about which one dare not speak. I cannot often trust myself to talk of her.'

I liked her better after this. At first her beauty and her handsome dress had seemed a little overpowering to me; I had felt as if she were a being of another order, a bright happy creature not subject to the common woes of life. But now that she had spoken of her own sorrows, I felt that we were upon a level; and I stole my hand timidly into hers, and murmured some apology for my previous rudeness.

'You were not rude, dear. I know I must have seemed very intrusive when I disturbed you; but I could not bear to hear you crying like that. And now tell me where you sleep.'

I described the room as well as I could.

'I know where you mean,' she said; 'it's close to my room. I have the privilege of a little room to myself, you know; and on half-holidays I have a fire there, and write my letters, or paint; and you must come and sit with me on those afternoons, and we can be as happy as possible together working and talking. Do you paint?'

'A little—in a schoolgirlish kind of way.'

'Quite as well as I do, I daresay,' Miss Darrell answered, laughing gaily, 'only you are more modest about it. O, here comes your supper; may I sit with you while you eat it?'

'I shall be very glad if you will.'

'I hope you have brought Miss Crofton a good supper, Sarah,' she went on in the same gay girlish way.—' Sarah is a very good creature, you must know, Miss Crofton, though she seems a little grim to strangers. That's only a way of hers: she *can* smile, I assure you, though you'd hardly think so.'

Sarah's hard-looking mouth expanded into a kind of grin at this.

'There's no getting over you, Miss Darrell,' she said; 'you've got such a way of your own. I've brought Miss Crofton some cold beef; but if she'd like a bit of pickle, I wouldn't mind going to ask cook for it. Cold meat does eat a little dry without pickle.'

This 'bit of pickle' was evidently a concession in my favour made to please Emily Darrell. I thanked Sarah, and told her that I would not trouble her with a journey to the cook. I was faint and worn-out with my day's pilgrimage, and had eaten very little since morning; but the most epicurean repast ever prepared by a French chef would have seemed so much dust and ashes to me that night; so I sat down meekly to my supper of bread and meat, and listened to Milly Darrell's chatter as I ate it.

Of course she told me all about the school, Miss Bagshot, and Miss Susan Bagshot. The elder of these two ladies was her favourite. Miss Susan had, in the remote period of her youth, been the victim of some unhappy love-affair, which had soured her disposition, and inclined her to look on the joys and follies of girlhood with a jaundiced eye. It was easy enough to please Miss Bagshot, who had a genial matronly way, and took real delight in her pupils; but it was almost impossible to satisfy Miss Susan.

'And I am sorry to say that you will be a good deal with her,' Miss Darrell said, shaking her head gravely; 'for you are to take the second English class under her—I heard them say so at dinner to-day—and I am afraid she will fidget you almost out of your life; but you must try to keep your temper, and take things as quietly as you can, and I daresay in time you will be able to get on with her.'

'I'm sure I hope so,' I answered rather sadly; and then Miss Darrell asked me how long I was to be at Albury Lodge.

'Three years,' I told her; 'and after that, Miss Bagshot is to place me somewhere as a governess.'

'You are going to be a governess always?'

'I suppose so,' I answered. The word 'always' struck me with a little sharp pain, almost like a wound. Yes, I supposed it would be always. I was neither pretty nor attractive. What issue could there be for me out of that dull hackneyed round of daily duties which makes up the sum of a governess's life?

'I am obliged to do something for my living,' I said; 'my father is very poor. I hope I may be able to help him a little by and by.'

'And my father is so ridiculously rich. He is a great ironmaster, and has wharves and warehouses, and goodness knows what, at North Shields. How hard it seems!'

'What seems hard?' I asked absently.

'That money should be so unequally divided. Do you know, I don't think I should much mind going out as a governess: it would be a way of seeing life. One must meet with all sorts of adventures, going among strangers like that.'

I looked at her as she smiled at me, with a smile that gave an indescribable brightness to her face, and I fancied that for her indeed there could be no form of life so dull that would not hold some triumph, some success. She seemed a creature born to extract brightness out of the commonest things, a creature to be only admired and caressed, go where she might.

'You a governess!' I said, a little scornfully; 'you are not of the clay that makes governesses.'

'Why not?'

'You are much too pretty and too fascinating.'

'O, Mary Crofton, Mary Crofton—may I call you Mary, please? we are going to be such friends—if you begin by flattering me like that, how am I ever to trust you and lean upon you? I want some one with a stronger mind than my own, you know, dear, to lead me right; for I'm the weakest, vainest creature in the world, I believe. Papa has spoiled me so.'

'If you are always like what you are to-night, I don't think the spoiling has done much mischief,' I said.

'O, I am always amiable enough, so long as I have my own way. And now tell me all about your home.'

I gave her a faithful account of my brothers and my sister, and a brief description of the dear old-fashioned cottage, with its white-plaster walls crossed with great black beams, its many gables and quaint latticed windows. I told her how happy and united we had always been at home, and how this made my separation from those I loved so much the harder to bear; to all of which Milly Darrell listened with most unaffected sympathy.

Early the next day my new life began in real earnest. Miss Susan Bagshot did not allow me to waste my time in idleness until the arrival of my pupils. She gave me a pile of exercises to correct, and some difficult needlework to finish; and I found I had indeed a sharp taskmistress in this blighted lady.

'Girls of your age are so incorrigibly idle,' she said; 'but I must give you to understand at once that you will have no time for dawdling at Albury Lodge. The first bell rings at a quarter before six, and at a quarter past I shall expect to see you in the schoolroom. You will superintend the younger pupils' pianoforte practice from that time till eight o'clock, at which hour we breakfast. From nine till twelve you will take the second division of the second class for English, according to the routine arranged by me, which you had better copy from a paper I will lend you for that purpose. After dinner you will take the same class for two hours' reading until four;

from four to five you will superintend the needlework class. Your evenings—with the exception of the careful correction of all the day's exercises—will be your own. I hope you have a sincere love of your vocation, Miss Crofton.'

I said that I hoped I should grow to like my work as I became accustomed to it. I had never yet tried teaching, except with my young sister and brothers. My heart sank as I remembered our free-and-easy studies in the sunny parlour at home, or out in the garden under the pink and white hawthorns sometimes on balmy mornings in the early summer.

Miss Susan shook her head doubtfully.

'Unless you have a love of your vocation you will never succeed, Miss Crofton,' she said solemnly.

I freely confess that this love she spoke of never came to me. I tried to do my duty, and I endured all the hardships of my life in, I hope, a cheerful spirit. But the dry monotony of the studies had no element of pleasantness, and I used to wonder how Miss Susan could derive pleasure—as it was evident she did—from the exercise of her authority over those hapless scholars who had the misfortune to belong to her class. Day after day they heard the same lectures, listened submissively to the same reproofs, and toiled on upon that bleak bare high-road to learning, along which it was her delight to drive them. Nothing like a flower brightened their weary way—it was all alike dust and barrenness; but they ploughed on dutifully, cramming their youthful minds with the hardest dates and facts to be found in the history of mankind, the dreariest statistics, the driest details of geography, and the most recondite rules of grammar, until the happy hour arrived in which they took their final departure from Albury Lodge, to forget all they had learnt there in the briefest possible time.

How my thoughts used to wander away sometimes as I sat at my desk, distracted by the unmelodious sound of Miss Susan's voice lecturing some victim in her own division at the next table, while one of the girls in mine droned drearily at Lingard, or Pinnock's *Goldsmith*, as the case might be! How the vision of my own bright home haunted me during those long monotonous afternoons, while the March winds made the poplars rock in the garden outside the schoolroom, or the April rain beat against the great bare windows!

CHAPTER II.

MILLY'S VISITOR.

It was not often that I had a half-holiday to myself, for Miss Susan Bagshot seemed to take a delight in finding me something to do on those occasions; but whenever I had, I spent it with Milly Darrell, and on these rare afternoons I was perfectly happy. I had grown to love her as I did not think it was in me to love any one who was not of my own flesh and blood; and in so loving her, I only returned the affection which she felt for me.

I am sure it was the fact of my friendlessness, and of my subordinate position in the school, which had drawn this girl's generous heart towards me; and I should have been hard indeed if I had not felt touched by her regard. She soon grew indescribably dear to me. She was of my own age, able to sympathise with every thought and fancy of mine; the frankest, most open-hearted of creatures; a little proud of her beauty, perhaps, when it was praised by those she loved, but never proud of her wealth, or insolent to those whose gifts were less than hers.

I used to write my home-letters in her room on these rare and happy afternoons, while she painted at an easel near the window. The room was small, but better furnished than the ordinary rooms in the house, and it was brightened by all sorts of pretty things,—handsomely-bound books upon hanging shelves, pictures, Dresden cups and saucers, toilet-bottles and boxes, which Miss Darrell had brought from home. Over the mantelpiece there was a large photograph of her father, and by the bedside there hung a more flattering water-coloured portrait, painted by Milly herself. It was a powerful and rather a handsome face, but I thought the expression a little hard and cold, even in Milly's portrait.

She painted well, and had a real love of art. Her studies at Albury Lodge were of rather a desultory kind, as she was not supposed to belong to any class; but she had lessons from nearly half-a-dozen different masters—German lessons, Italian lessons, drawing lessons, music and singing lessons—and was altogether a very profitable pupil. She had her own way with every one, I found, and I believe Miss Bagshot was really fond of her.

Her father was travelling in Italy at this time, and did not often write to her—a fact that distressed her very much, I know; but she used to shake off her sorrow in a bright hopeful way that was peculiar to her, always making excuses for the dilatory correspondent. She loved him intensely, and keenly felt this separation from him; but the doctors had recommended him rest and change of air and scene, she told me, and she was glad to think he was obeying them.

Upon one of these half-holidays, when midsummer was near at hand, we were interrupted by an unwonted event, in the shape of a visit from a cousin of Milly's; a young man who occupied an important position in her father's house of business, and of whom she had sometimes talked to me, but not much. His name was Julian Stormont, and he was the only son of Mr. Darrell's only sister, long since dead.

It was a sultry afternoon, and we were spending it in a rustic summer-house at the end of a broad gravel walk that went the whole length of the large garden. Milly had her drawing materials on the table before her, but had not been using them. I was busy with a piece of fancy-work which Miss Susan Bagshot had given me to finish. We were sitting like this, when my old acquaintance Sarah, the housemaid, came to announce a visitor for Miss Darrell.

Milly sprang to her feet, flushed with excitement.

'It must be papa!' she cried joyfully.

'Lor', no, miss; don't you go to excite yourself like that. It isn't your pa; it's a younger gentleman.'

She handed Milly a card.

'Mr. Stormont!' the girl exclaimed, with a disappointed air; 'my cousin Julian. I am coming to him, of course, Sarah. But I wish you had given me the card at once.'

'Won't you go and do somethink to your hair, miss? most young ladies do.'

'O yes, I know; there are girls who would stop to have their hair done in Grecian plaits, if the dearest friend they had in the world was waiting for them in the drawing-room. My hair will do well enough, Sarah.—Come, Mary, you'll come to the house with me, won't you?'

'Lor', miss, here comes the gentleman,' said Sarah; and then decamped by an obscure side-path.

'I had better leave you to see him alone, Milly,' I said; but she told me imperatively to stay, and I stayed.

She went a little way to meet the gentleman, who seemed pleased to see her, but whom she received rather coldly, as I thought. But I had not long to think about it, before she had brought him to the summer-house, and introduced him to me.

'My cousin Julian—Miss Crofton.'

He bowed rather stiffly, and then seated himself by his cousin's side, and put his hat upon the table before him. I had plenty of time to look at him as he sat there talking of all sorts of things connected with Thornleigh, and Miss Darrell's friends in that neighbourhood. He was very good-looking, fair and pale, with regular well-cut features, and rather fine blue eyes; but I fancied those clear blue eyes had a cold look, and that there was an expression of iron will about the mouth and powerful prominent chin. The upper part of the face was thoughtful, and there were lines already on the high white forehead, from which the thin straight chestnut hair was carefully brushed. It was the face of a very clever man, I thought; but I was not so sure that it was the face of a man I could like, or whom I should be inclined to trust.

Mr. Stormont had a low pleasant voice and an agreeable manner of speaking. His way of treating his cousin was half deferential, half playful; but once, when I looked up suddenly from my work, I seemed to catch a glimpse of a deeper meaning in the cold blue eyes—a look of singular intensity fixed on Milly's bright face.

Whatever this look might mean, she was unconscious of it; she went on talking gaily of Thornleigh and her Thornleigh friends.

'I do so want to come home, Julian,' she said. 'Do you think there is any hope for me this midsummer?'

'I think there is every hope. I think it is almost certain you will come home.'

'O Julian, how glad I am!'

'But suppose there should be a surprise for you when you come home, Milly,—a change that you may not quite like, at first?'

'What change?'

'Has your father told you nothing?'

'Nothing, except about his journeys from place to place, and not much about them. He has written very seldom during the last six months.'

'He has been too much engaged, I suppose; and it's rather like him to have said nothing about it. How would you like a stepmother, Milly?'

She gave a little cry, and grew suddenly pale.

'Papa has married again!' she said.

Julian Stormont drew a newspaper from his pocket, and laid it before her, pointing to an announcement in one column:

'On May 18th, at the English Legation in Paris, William Darrell, Esq., of Thornleigh, Yorkshire, to Augusta, daughter of the late Theodore Chester, Esq., of Regent's Park.'

He read this aloud very slowly, watching Milly's pale face as he read.

'There is no reason why this should distress you, my dear child,' he said. 'It was only to be expected that your father would marry again, sooner or later.'

'I have lost him!' she cried piteously.

'Lost him!'

'Yes; he can never be again the same to me that he has been. His new wife will come between us. No, Julian, I am not jealous. I do not grudge him his happiness, if this marriage can make him happy. I only feel that I have lost him for ever.'

'My dear Milly, that is utterly unreasonable. Your father told me most particularly to assure you of his unaltered affection, when I broke the news of this marriage to you. He was naturally a little nervous about doing it himself.'

'You must never let him know what I have said, Julian. He will never hear any expression of regret from me; and I will try to do my duty to this strange lady. Have you seen her yet?'

'No, they have not come home yet. They were in Switzerland when I heard of them last; but they are expected in a week or two. Come, my dear Milly, don't look so serious. I trust this marriage may turn out for your happiness, as well as for your father's. Rely upon it, you will find no change in his feelings towards you.'

'He will always be kind and good to me, I know,' she answered sadly. 'It is not possible for him to be anything but that; but I can never be his companion again as I have been. There is an end to all that.'

'That was a kind of association which could not be supposed to last all your life, Milly. It is to be hoped that somebody else will have a claim upon your companionship before many years have gone by.'

'I suppose you mean that I shall marry,' she said, looking at him with supreme indifference.

'Something like that, Milly.'

'I have always fancied myself living all my life with papa. I have never thought it possible that I could care for any one but him.'

Julian Stormont's face darkened a little, and he sat silent for some minutes, folding and refolding the newspaper in a nervous way.

'You are not very complimentary to your admirers at Thornleigh,' he said at last, with a short hoarse laugh.

'Who is there at Thornleigh? Have I really any admirers there?'

'I think I could name half-a-dozen.'

'Never mind them just now. I want you to tell me all you know about my stepmother.'

'That amounts to very little. All I can tell you is, that she is the daughter of a gentleman, highly accomplished, without money, and four-and-twenty years of age. She was travelling as companion to an elderly lady when your father met her in a picture-gallery at Florence. He knew the old lady, I believe, and by that means became acquainted with the younger one.'

'Only four-and-twenty! only four years older than I!'

'Rather young, is it not? but when a man of your father's age makes a second marriage, he is apt to marry a young woman. Of course this is quite a love-match.'

'Yes, quite a love-match,' Milly repeated, with a sigh.

I knew she could not help that natural pang of jealousy, as she thought how she and her father had once been all the world to each other. She had told me so often of their happy companionship, the perfect confidence that had existed between them.

Julian Stormont sat talking to her—and a little, a very little, to me—for about half an hour longer, and then departed. He was to sleep at Fendale, and go back to North Shields next morning. He was his uncle's right hand in the business, Milly told me; and from the little I had seen of him I could fancy him a power in any sphere.

'Papa has a very high opinion of him,' she said, when we were talking of him after he had left us.

'And you like him very much, I suppose?'

'O yes, I like him very well. I have known him all my life. We are almost like brother and sister; only Julian is one of those thoughtful reserved persons one does not get on with very fast.'

CHAPTER III.

AT THORNLEIGH.

THE midsummer holidays began at last, and Mr. Darrell came in person to fetch his daughter, much to her delight. She was not to return to school any more unless she liked, he told her. Her new mamma was most anxious to receive her, and she could have masters at Thornleigh to complete her education, if it were not already finished.

Her eyes were full of tears when she came to tell me this, and carry me off to the drawing-room to introduce me to her father, an introduction she insisted upon making in spite of my entreaties,—for I was rather shy at this period of my life, and dreaded an encounter with a stranger.

Mr. Darrell received me most graciously. He was a tall fine-looking man, very like the photograph in Milly's bedroom, and I detected the hard look about the mouth which I had noticed in both portraits. He seemed remarkably fond of his daughter; and I have never seen a prettier picture than she made as she stood beside him, clinging to his arm, and looking lovingly up at him with her dark hazel eyes.

He asked me where I was to spend my holidays; and on hearing that I was to stay at Albury Lodge, asked whether I would like to come to Thornleigh with Milly for the midsummer vacation. My darling clapped her hands gaily as he made this offer, and cried:

'O yes, Mary, you will come, won't you?—You dear kind papa, that is just like you, always able to guess what one wishes. There is nothing in the world I should like better than to have Mary at Thornleigh.'

'Then you have only to pack a box with all possible expedition, and to come away with us, Miss Crofton,' said Mr. Darrell; 'the train starts in an hour and a half. I can only give you an hour.'

I thanked him as well as I could—awkwardly enough, I daresay—for his kindness, and ran away to ask Miss Bagshot's consent to the visit. This she gave readily, in spite of some objections suggested by Miss Susan, and I had nothing more to do than to pack my few dresses—my two coloured muslins, a white dress for festive occasions, a black-silk dress which was preeminently my 'best,' and some print morning-dresses—wondering as I packed them how these things would pass current among the grandeurs of Thornleigh. All this was finished well within the hour, and I put on my bonnet and shawl, and ran down—flushed with hurry and excitement, and very happy—to join my friends in the drawing-room.

Miss Bagshot was there, talking of her attachment to her sweet young friend, and her regret at losing her. Mr. Darrell cut these lamentations short when he found that I was ready, and we drove off to the station in the fly that had brought him to Albury Lodge.

I looked at the little station to-day with a very different feeling from that dull despondency which had possessed me six months before, when I arrived there in the bleak January weather. The thought of five weeks' respite from the monotonous routine of Albury Lodge was almost perfect happiness. I did not forget those I loved at home, or cease to regret the poverty that prevented my going home for the holidays; but since this was impossible, nothing could have been pleasanter than the idea of the visit I was going to pay.

Throughout the journey Mr. Darrell was all that

was gracious and kind. He talked a good deal of his wife; dwelling much upon her accomplishments and amiability, and assuring his daughter again and again that she could not fail to love her.

'I was a little bit of a coward in the business, I confess, Milly,' he said, in the midst of this talk, 'and hadn't courage to tell you anything till the deed was done; and then I thought it was as well to let Julian make the announcement.'

'You ought to have trusted me better, papa,' Milly said tenderly; and I knew what perfect self-abnegation there was in the happy smile with which she gave him her hand.

'And you are not angry with me, my darling?' he asked.

'Angry with you, papa? as if I had any right to be angry with you! Only try to love me a little, as you used to do, and I shall be quite happy.'

'I shall never love you less, my dear.'

The journey was not a long one; and the country through which we passed was very fair to look upon in the bright June afternoon. The landscape changed when we were within about thirty miles of our destination: the fertile farmlands and waving fields of green corn gave place to an open moor, and

I felt from far off the fresh breath of the ocean. This broad undulating moorland was new to me, and I thought there was a wild kind of beauty in its loneliness. As for Milly, she looked out at the moor with rapture, and strained her eyes to catch the first glimpse of the hills about Thornleigh—those hills of which she had talked to me so often in her little room at school.

The station we had to stop at was ten miles from Mr. Darrell's house, and a barouche-and-pair was waiting for us in the sunny road outside. We drove along a road that crossed the moor, until we came to a little village of scattered houses, with a fine old church—at one end of which an ancient sacristy seemed mouldering slowly to decay. We drove past the gates of two or three rather important houses, lying half-hidden in their gardens, and then turned sharply off into a road that went up a hill, nearly at the top of which we came to a pair of noble old carved iron gates, surmounted with a coat-of-arms, and supported on each side by massive stone pillars, about which the ivy twined lovingly.

An old man came out of a pretty rustic-looking lodge and opened these gates, and we drove through an avenue of some extent, which led straight to the front of the house, the aspect of which delighted me. It was very old and massively built, and had quite a baronial look, I thought. There was a wide stone terrace with ponderous moss-grown stone balustrades round three sides of it, and at each angle a broad flight of steps leading down to a second terrace, with sloping green banks that melted into the turf of the lawn. The house stood on the summit of a hill, and from one side commanded a noble view of the sea.

A lady came out of the curious old stone porch as the carriage drove up, and stood at the top of the terrace steps waiting for us. I guessed immediately that this must be Mrs. Darrell.

Milly hung back a little shyly, as her father led her up the steps with her hand through his arm. She was very pale, and I could see that she was trembling. Mrs. Darrell came forward to her quickly, and kissed her.

'My darling Emily,' she cried, 'I am so delighted to see you at last.—O William, you did not deceive me when you promised me a beautiful daughter.'

Milly blushed, and smiled at this compliment, but still clung to her father, with shy downcast eyes.

I had time to look at Mrs. Darrell while this introduction was being made. She was not by any means a beautiful woman, but she was what I suppose would have been called eminently interesting. She was tall and slim, very graceful-looking, with a beautiful throat and a well-shaped head. Her features, with the exception of her eyes, were in no way remarkable; but those were sufficiently striking to give character to a face that might otherwise have been insipid. They were large luminous gray eyes, with black lashes, and rather strongly-marked brows of a much darker brown than her hair. That was of a nondescript shade, neither auburn nor chestnut, and with little light or colour in its soft silky masses; but it seemed to harmonise very well with her pale complexion. Lavater has warned us to distrust any one whose hair and eyebrows are of a different colour. I remembered this as I looked at Mrs. Darrell.

She was dressed in white; and I fancied the transparent muslin dress, with no other ornament than a lilac ribbon at the waist, was peculiarly becoming to her slender figure and delicate face. Her husband seemed to think so too, for he looked at her with a fond admiring glance as he offered her his arm to return to the house.

'I mustn't forget to introduce Miss Crofton to

you, Augusta,' he said; 'a school friend of Milly's, who has kindly accepted my invitation to spend the holidays with her.'

Mrs. Darrell gave me her hand; but I fancied that she did so rather coldly, and I had an uneasy sense that I was not very welcome to the new mistress of Thornleigh.

'You will find your old rooms all ready for you, Milly,' she said; 'I suppose we had better put Miss Crofton in the blue room—next yours?'

'If you please, Mrs. Darrell.'

'What, Milly, won't you call me mamma?'

Milly was silent for a few moments, with a pained expression in her face.

'Pray, forgive me,' she said in a low voice; 'I cannot call any one by that name.'

Augusta Darrell kissed her again silently.

'It shall be as you wish, dear,' she said, after a pause.

A rosy-cheeked, pleasant-looking girl, who had been accustomed to wait on Milly in the old time, came forward to meet us, and ran before us to our rooms, expressing her delight at her young lady's return all the way she went.

The rooms were very pretty, and were situated

in that portion of the house which looked towards the sea. There was a sitting-room, brightly furnished with some light kind of wood, and with chintz hangings all over rose-buds and butterflies. This had been Milly's schoolroom, and there were a good many books in two pretty-looking bookcases on each side of the fireplace. Besides these, there were some curious old cabinets full of shells and china. It was altogether the prettiest, most homelike room one could imagine.

Opening out of this, there was a large airy bedroom, with three windows commanding that glorious view of moorland and sea; and beyond that, a dainty little dressing-room. The next door in the corridor opened into the room that had been allotted to me; a large comfortable-looking room, in which there was an old-fashioned mahogany four-post bed with blue-damask curtains.

I went to Milly's dressing-room when my own simple toilet was finished, and stood by the open window talking to her while she arranged her hair. She dismissed her little maid directly I went into the room, and I felt she had something to say to me.

'Well, Mary,' she began at once, 'what do you think of her?'

'Of Mrs. Darrell?'

'Of course.'

'What opinion can I possibly form about her, after seeing her for three minutes, Milly? I think she is very elegant-looking. That is the only idea I have about her yet.'

'Do you think she looks *true*, Mary? Do you think she has married papa because she loves him?'

'My dear child, how can I tell that? She is a great many years younger than your papa, but I do not see that the difference between them need be any real hindrance to her loving him. He is a man whom any woman might care for, I should think; to say nothing of her natural gratitude towards the man who has rescued her from a position of dependence.'

'Gratitude is all nonsense,' Miss Darrell answered impatiently. 'I want to know that my father is loved as he deserves to be loved. I shall never tolerate that woman unless I can feel sure of that.'

'I believe you are prejudiced against her already, Milly,' I said reproachfully.

'I daresay I am, Mary. I daresay I feel unjustly about her; but I don't like her face.'

'What is there in her face that you don't like?'

'O, I can't tell you that—an undefinable something. I have a sort of conviction that she and I can never love each other.'

'It is rather hard upon Mrs. Darrell to begin with such a feeling as that, Milly.'

'I can't help it. Of course I shall try to do my duty to her, for papa's sake, and I shall do my best to conquer all these unchristian feelings. But we cannot command our hearts, you know, Mary, and I don't think I shall ever love my stepmother.'

She took me down to the drawing-room after this. It was half-past six, and we were to dine at seven. The drawing-room was a long room, with five windows opening on to the terrace, an old-fashioned-looking room with panelled walls and a fine arched ceiling. The wainscot was painted white, with gilt mouldings, and the cornice and architraves of the doors were elaborately carved. The furniture was white-and-gold like the walls, and in that spurious classical style which prevailed during the first French Empire. The window-curtains and coverings of sofas and chairs were of dark-green velvet.

A gentleman was standing in one of the open windows looking out at the garden. He turned as Milly and I went in, and I recognised Mr. Stormont.

He came forward to shake hands with his cousin, and smiled his peculiar slow smile at her expression of surprise.

'You didn't know I was here, Milly?'

'No, indeed; I had no idea of seeing you.'

'I wonder your father did not tell you of my visit. I came over this morning for a fortnight's holiday. I've been working a little harder than usual lately, and my uncle is good enough to say I have earned a rest.'

'I wonder you don't go abroad for a change.'

'I don't care about a change. I had much rather come to Thornleigh.'

He looked at her very earnestly as he said this. I had been sure of it that afternoon when we all three sat in the summer-house at Albury Lodge, but I could see that Milly herself had no idea of the truth.

'Well, Milly, what do you think of your new mamma?' he asked presently.

'I had rather not tell you yet.'

'Humph! that hardly sounds favourable to the lady. She seems to me a very charming person; but she is not my stepmother, and, of course, that makes a difference. Your father is intensely devoted.'

Mr. Darrell came into the room a few minutes

after this, and his wife followed him almost immediately. Milly placed herself next her father, and contrived to absorb his attention, not quite to the satisfaction of the elder lady, I fancied. Those bright gray eyes flashed upon my darling with a brief look of anger, which changed in the next moment to quiet watchfulness.

Mrs. Darrell stood by one of the tables, idly turning over some books and papers, and finding me seated near her, began to talk to me presently in a very gracious manner, asking me how I liked Thornleigh, and a few other questions of a stereotyped kind; but even while she talked those watchful eyes were always turned towards the window where the father and daughter stood side by side. Mr. Stormont came over to her while she was talking to me, and joined in the conversation; in the midst of which a grave gray-haired old butler came to announce dinner.

Mr. Stormont offered his arm to the lady of the house, while Mr. Darrell gave one arm to me and the other to his daughter; and we went down a long passage, at the end of which was the dining-room, a noble old room, with dark oak panelling and a great many pictures by the old masters, which were, no doubt, as valuable as they were dingy. We dined at an oval table, prettily decorated with flowers and with some very curious old silver.

There was a good deal of talk at dinner, in which I could take very little part. Mr. and Mrs. Darrell talked to Julian Stormont of their travels; and I must confess the lady talked well, with no affectation of enthusiasm, and with an evident knowledge and appreciation of the things she was speaking about. I envied her those wanderings in sunny foreign lands, even though they had been made in the company of an invalid dowager, and I wondered whether she would be happy in a settled existence at Thornleigh.

After dinner Milly took me out upon the terrace, and from thence we went to explore the gardens. We had not been out long before Julian Stormont came to join us. We had been talking pleasantly enough till he appeared, but his coming seemed to make us both silent, and he himself had a thoughtful air. I watched his pale face as he walked beside us in the twilight, and was again struck by the careworn look about the brow and the resolute expression of the mouth.

He was very fond of Milly. Of that fact there could be no possible doubt; and I think he had already begun to suffer keenly from the knowledge that his love was unreturned. That he hoped against hope at this time—that he counted fully on his power to win her in the future, I know. He was too wise to precipitate matters by any untimely avowal of his feelings. He waited with a quiet resolute patience which was a part of his nature.

Of course we talked a little, but it was in a straggling, desultory kind of way; and I think it was a relief to all of us when we finished the round of the gardens and went in through one of the drawing-room windows. The room was lighted with lamps and candles placed about upon the tables, and Mrs. Darrell was sitting near her husband, employed upon some airy scrap of fancy-work, while he read his *Times*.

He asked for some music soon after we went in, and she rose to obey him with a very charming air of submission. She played magnificently, with a power and style that were quite new to me, for I had heard no professional performers. She sang an Italian scena afterwards, in a rich mezzo-soprano, and with a kind of suppressed passion that impressed me deeply. I scarcely wondered, after hearing her play and sing, that Mr. Darrell had been fascinated by her. These gifts of hers were in themselves sufficient to subjugate a man who really cared for music.

Milly was charmed into forgetfulness of her prejudices. She went over to the piano and kissed her stepmother.

'Papa told me how clever you were,' she said; 'but he did not tell me you were a genius.'

Mrs. Darrell received the compliment very modestly, and then tried to persuade Milly to sing or play; but the girl declined resolutely. Nothing could induce her to touch the piano after that brilliant performance.

The next day and several days passed very quietly, and in a kind of monotonous comfort. The rector of the parish dined with us one day, and on another a neighbouring squire with his wife and three daughters. Milly and I spent a good deal of our time in the gardens and on the sea-shore, with Julian Stormont for our companion, while Mr. and Mrs. Darrell rode or drove together. My darling could see that she was not expected to join them in these rides and drives, and I think this confirmed her idea that her father was in a manner lost to her.

'I must try to be satisfied with this new state of things, Mary,' she said, with a sigh of resignation.

'If my father is happy, I ought to be contented. But O, my dear, if you could have seen us together a year ago, you would know how much I have lost.'

I had been at Thornleigh a little more than a week, when Mr. Darrell one morning proposed a drive to a place called Cumber Priory, which was one of the show-houses of the neighbourhood. It was a very old place, he said, and had been one of the earliest monastic settlements in that part of the country. Milly and her father and her cousin had been there a great many times, and the visit was proposed for the gratification of Mrs. Darrell and myself.

She assented graciously, as she always did to every proposition of her husband's, and we started soon after breakfast in the barouche, with Julian Stormont on horseback. The drive was delightful; for, after leaving the hilly district about Thornleigh, our road lay through a wood, where the trees were of many hundred years' growth. I recognised groups of oak and beech that I had seen among the sketches in Milly's portfolio.

On the other side of the wood we came to some dilapidated-looking gates, with massive stone escutcheons on the great square pillars. There was a lodge, but it was evidently unoccupied, and Mr. Darrell's footman got down from the box to open the gates. Within we made the circuit of a neglected lawn, divided from a park by a sunk fence, across which some cattle stared at us in a lazy manner as we drove past them. The house was a long low building with heavily mullioned windows, and was flanked by gothic towers. Most of the windows had closed shutters, and the place had altogether a deserted look.

'The Priory has not been occupied for several years,' Mr. Darrell said, as if in answer to my thoughts as I looked up at the closed windows. 'The family have been too poor to live in it in anything like their old state. There is only one member of the old family remaining now, and he leads a wandering kind of life abroad, I believe.'

'What has made them so poor?' asked Mrs. Darrell.

'Extravagant habits, I suppose,' answered her husband, with an expressive shrug of the shoulders. 'The Egertons have always been a wild race.'

'Egerton!' Mrs. Darrell repeated; 'I thought the name of these people was Cumber.'

'No; Cumber is only the name of the place. It has been in the Egerton family for centuries.'

'Indeed!'

I was seated exactly opposite her, and I was surprised by the strange startled look in her face as she repeated the name of Egerton. That look passed away in the next moment, and left her with her usual air of languid indifference; a placid kind of listlessness which harmonised very well with her pale complexion and delicate features. She was not a woman from whom one expected much animation.

The low iron-studded door of the Priory was opened by a decent-looking old woman of that species which seems created expressly for the showing of old houses. She divined our errand at once, and as soon as we were in the hall, began her catalogue of pictures and curiosities in the usual mechanical way, while we looked about us, always fixing our eyes on the wrong object, and more bewildered than enlightened by her description of the chief features of the place.

We went from room to room, the dame throwing open the shutters of the deep-set gothic windows, and letting in a flood of sunshine upon the faded tapestries and tarnished picture-frames. It was a noble old place, and the look of decay upon everything was more in accord with its grandeur than any modern splendour could have been.

We had been through all the rooms on the ground floor, most of which opened into one another, and were returning towards the hall, when Mr. Darrell missed his wife, and sent me back to look for her in one direction, while he went in another. I hurried through three or four empty rooms, until I came to a small one at the end of the house, and here I found her. I had not noticed this room much, for it was furnished in a more modern style than the rest of the house, and the old housekeeper had made very light of it, hurrying us back to look at some armour over the chimneypiece in the next room. It was her master's study, she had said, and was not generally shown to strangers.

It was a small dark-looking room, lined with dingily-bound books upon heavy carved-oak shelves, and with no other furniture than a massive writing-table and three or four arm-chairs. Over the mantelpiece, which was modern and low, there was a portrait of a young man with a dark handsome face, and it was at this that Augusta Darrell was looking. I could see her face in profile as she stood upon the hearth with her clenched hand upon the mantelpiece, and I had never before seen such an expression in any human countenance.

What was it? Despair, remorse, regret? I know not; but it was a look of keenest anguish, of unutterable sorrow. The face was deadly pale, the great gray eyes looking upwards at the portrait, the lips locked together rigidly.

She did not hear my footstep; it was only when I spoke to her that she turned towards me with a stony face, and asked what I wanted.

I told her that Mr. Darrell had sent me.

'I was coming this instant,' she said, resuming her usual manner with an effort. 'I had only loitered to look at that portrait. A fine face, is it not, Miss Crofton?'

'A handsome one, at any rate,' I answered doubtfully, for that dark haughty countenance struck me as rather repellent than attractive.

'That's as much as to say you don't think it a good face. Well, perhaps you are right. It reminded me of some one I knew a long time ago, and was rather interesting to me on that account. And then I fell into a kind of a reverie, and forgot that my dear husband might miss me.'

He came into the room as she was saying this. She told him that she had stopped to look at the portrait, and asked whose it was.

'It is a likeness of Angus Egerton, the present owner of the Priory,' Mr. Darrell answered; 'and a very good likeness, too—of as bad a man as ever lived, I believe,' he added in a lower voice.

'A bad man?'

'Yes; he broke his mother's heart.'

'In what manner?'

'He fell in love with a girl of low birth, whom he met in the course of a pedestrian tour in the West of England, and was going to marry her, I believe, when Mrs. Egerton got wind of the affair. She was a very proud woman—one of the most resolute masculine-minded women I ever knew. She went down into Devonshire where the girl lived immediately, and by some means or other prevented the marriage. How it was done I never heard; but it was not until a year afterwards that Angus Egerton discovered his mother's part in the business. He came down to the Priory suddenly and unexpectedly at a late hour one night, and walked straight to his mother's room. I have heard that old woman who has been showing us the house describe his ghastly face—she was Mrs. Egerton's maid in those days—as he pushed her aside and went into the room where his mother was sitting. There was a dreadful scene between them, and at the end of it Angus Egerton walked out of the house, swearing never again to enter it while his mother lived. He has kept his word. Mrs. Egerton never crossed the threshold after that night, and refused to see anybody except her servants and her doctor. She lived this lonely kind of life for nearly three years, and then died of some slow wasting disease, for which the doctor could find no name.'

'And where did Mr. Egerton go after leaving her that night?'

'He slept at a little inn at Cumber, and went back to London next morning. He left England soon after that, and has lived abroad ever since.'

'And you think him a very bad man?'

'I consider his conduct to his mother a sufficient evidence of that.'

'He may have believed himself deeply wronged.'

'He must have known that she had acted in his interests when she prevented his committing the folly of a low marriage. She was his mother, and had been a most devoted and indulgent mother.'

'And in the end contrived to break his heart—to say nothing of the girl who loved him, who was of course a piece of common clay, not worth consideration.'

'I did not think you had so much romance, Augusta,' said Mr. Darrell, laughing; 'I suppose it is natural for a woman to take the part of unfortunate lovers, however foolish the affair may be. But I believe this Devonshire girl was quite unworthy of an honourable attachment on the part of any man. You see I knew and liked Mrs. Egerton, and I know how she loved her son. I cannot forgive him his conduct to her; nor have the reports of his life abroad been by any means favourable to his character. His career seems to have been a very wild and dissipated one.'

'And he has never married?'

'No, he has never married.'

'He has been true, at least,' Mrs. Darrell said in a low thoughtful voice.

We had lingered in the little study while her husband had told his story. We went back to the hall now, and found Milly and Mr. Stormont looking rather listlessly at the old portraits of the Egerton race. I was anxious to see a picture of the last Mrs. Egerton, after what I had heard about her, and, at my request, the housekeeper showed me one in the drawing-room.

She was very handsome, and wonderfully like her

son. I could fancy those two haughty spirits in opposition.

We spent another hour looking over the rest of the house—old tapestry, old pictures, old china, old furniture, secret staircases, carved chimneypieces, muniment chests, and the usual objects of interest to be found in such a place. After that we walked a little in the neglected garden, where there were old holly hedges that had grown high and wild for want of clipping, and where a curious old sun-dial had fallen down upon the grass in a forlorn way. The paths were all green and moss-grown, and the roses were almost choked with bindweed. I saw Mrs. Darrell gather one of these roses and put it in her breast. It was the first time I had ever seen her pluck a flower, though there was a wealth of roses at Thornleigh.

So ended our visit to Cumber Priory; a place that was destined to be very memorable to some of us in the time to come.

CHAPTER IV.

MRS. THATCHER.

IT had been Milly's habit to devote one day a week to visiting among the poor, before she went to Albury Lodge; and she now resumed this practice, I accompanying her upon her visits. I had been used to going about among the cottagers at home, and I liked the work. It was very pleasant to see Milly Darrell with these people—the perfect confidence and sympathy between them and her, the delight they seemed to take in her bright cheering presence. I was struck by their simple natural manner, and the absence of anything like sycophancy to be observed in them. One day, when we had been to several cottages about the village, Milly asked me if I could manage rather a long walk; and on my telling her that I could, we started upon a lonely road that wound across the moor in a direction I had never walked in until that day. We went on for about two miles without passing a human habitation, and then came to one of the most desolate-looking cottages I ever remember seeing. It was little better than a cabin, and consisted only of two rooms—a kind of kitchen or dwelling-room, and a dark little bedchamber opening out of it.

'I am not going to introduce you to a very agreeable person, Mary,' Milly said, when we were within a few paces of this solitary dwelling; 'but old Rebecca is a character in her way, and I make a point of coming to see her now and then, though she is not always very gracious to me.'

It was a warm bright summer's day, but the door and the single window of the cottage were firmly closed. Milly knocked with her hand, and a thin feeble old voice called to her to 'come in.'

We went in: the atmosphere of the place was hot, and had an unpleasant doctor's-shoppish kind of odour, which I found was caused by some herbs in a jar that was simmering over a little stove in a corner. Bunches of dried herbs hung from the low ceiling, and on an old-fashioned lumbering chest of drawers that stood in the window there were more herbs and roots laid out to dry.

'Mrs. Thatcher is a very clever doctor, Mary,' said Milly, as if by way of introduction; 'all our servants come to her to be cured when they have colds and coughs.—And how are you this lovely summer weather, Mrs. Thatcher?'

'None too well, miss,' grumbled the old woman; 'I don't like the summer time; it never suited me.'

'That's strange,' said Milly gaily; 'I thought everybody liked summer.'

'Not those that live as I do, Miss Darrell. There's no illness in summer—no colds, nor coughs, nor sore-throats, nor suchlikes. I don't know that I shouldn't starve outright, if it wasn't for the ague; and even that is nothing now to what it used to be.'

I was quite horror-struck by this ghoulish speech; but Milly only laughed gaily at the old woman's candour.

'If the doctors were as plain-spoken as you, I daresay they'd say pretty much the same kind of thing, Mrs. Thatcher,' she said. 'How's your grandson?'

'O, he's well enough, Miss Darrell. Naught's never in danger.—Peter, come here, and see the young ladies.'

A poor, feeble, pale-faced, semi-idiotic-looking boy came slowly out of the dark little bedroom, and stood grinning at us. He had the white sickly aspect of a creature reared without the influence of air and light; and I pitied him intensely as he stood there staring and grinning in that dreadful hopeless manner.

'Poor Peter! He's no better, I'm afraid,' said Milly gently.

'No, miss, nor never will be. He knows more than people think, and has queer cunning ways of his own; but he'll never be any better or wiser than he is now.'

'Not if you were to take as much pains with him as you do with the patients who pay you, Mrs. Thatcher?' asked Milly.

'I've taken pains with him,' answered the woman, with a scowl. 'I took to him kindly enough when he was a little fellow; but he's grown up to be nothing but a plague and a burden to me.'

The boy left off grinning, and his poor weak chin sank lower on his narrow chest. His attitude had been a stooping one from the first; but he drooped visibly under the old woman's reproof.

'Can he employ himself in no way?'

'No, miss; except in picking the herbs and roots for me sometimes. He can do that, and he knows one from t'other.'

'He's of some use to you, at any rate, then,' said Milly.

'Little enough,' the old woman answered sulkily. 'I don't want help; I've plenty of time to gather them myself. But I've taught him to pick them, and it's the only thing he ever could learn.'

'Poor fellow! He's your only grandchild, isn't he, Mrs. Thatcher?'

'Yes, he's the only one, miss, and he'd need be. I don't know how I should keep another. You can't remember my daughter Ruth? She was as pretty a girl as you'd care to see. She was housemaid at Cumber Priory in Mrs. Egerton's time, and she married the butler. They set up in business in a little public-house in Thornleigh village, and he took to drinking, till everything went to rack and ruin. My poor girl took the trouble to heart more than her husband did, a great deal; and I believe it was the trouble that killed her. She died three weeks after that boy was born, and her husband ran away the day after her funeral, and has never been heard of since. Some say he drowned himself in the Clem; but he was a precious deal too fond of himself for that. He was up to his eyes in debt, and didn't leave a sixpence behind him; that's how Peter came to be thrown on my hands.'

'Come here, Peter,' said Milly softly; and the boy went to her directly, and took the hand she offered him.

'You've not forgotten me, have you, Peter? Miss Darrell, who used to talk to you sometimes a long time ago.'

The boy's vacant face brightened into something like intelligence.

'I know you, miss,' he said; 'you was always kind to Peter. It's not many that I know; but I know you.'

She took out her purse and gave him half-a-crown.

'There, Peter, there's a big piece of silver for your own self, to buy whatever you like—sugar-sticks, gingerbread, marbles—anything.'

His clumsy hand closed upon the coin, and I have no doubt he was pleased by the donation; but he never took his eyes from Milly Darrell's face. That bright lovely face seemed to exercise a kind of fascination upon him.

'Don't you think Peter would be better if you were to give him a little more air and sunshine,

Mrs. Thatcher?' Milly asked presently; 'that bedroom seems rather a dark close place.'

'He needn't be there unless he likes,' Mrs. Thatcher answered indifferently. 'He sits out of doors whenever he chooses.'

'Then I should always sit out-of-doors on fine days, if I were you, Peter,' said Milly.

After this she talked a little to Mrs. Thatcher, who was by no means a sympathetic person, while I sat looking on, and contemplating the old woman with a feeling that was the reverse of admiration.

She was of a short squat figure, with broad shoulders and no throat to speak of, and her head seemed too big for her body. Her face was long and thin, with large features, and a frame of scanty gray hair, among which a sandy tinge still lingered here and there; her eyes were of an ugly reddish-brown, and had, I thought, a most sinister expression. I must have been very ill, and sorely at a loss for a doctor, before I could have been induced to trust my health to the care of Mrs. Rebecca Thatcher.

I told Milly as much while we were walking homewards, and she admitted that Rebecca Thatcher was no favourite even among the country people, who believed implicitly in her skill.

'I'm afraid she tells fortunes, and dabbles in all sorts of superstitious tricks,' Milly added gravely; 'but she is so artful, there is no way of finding her out in that kind of business. The foolish country girls who consult her always keep her secret, and she manages to put on a fair face before our rector and his curate, who believe her to be a very respectable woman.'

The days and weeks slipped by very pleasantly at Thornleigh, and the end of those bright midsummer holidays came only too soon. It seemed a bitter thing to say 'good-bye' to Milly Darrell, and to go back alone to a place which must needs be doubly dull and dreary to me without her. She had been my only friend at Albury Lodge; loving her as I did, I had never cared to form any other friendship.

The dreaded day came at last—dreaded I know by both of us; and I said 'good-bye' to my darling so quietly, that I am sure none could have guessed the grief I felt in this parting. Mrs. Darrell was very kind and gracious on this occasion, begging that I would come back to Thornleigh at Christmas —if they should happen to spend their Christmas there.

Milly looked up at her wonderingly as she said this.

'Is there any chance of our spending it elsewhere, Augusta?' she asked.

Mrs. Darrell had persuaded her stepdaughter to use this familiar Christian name, rather than the more formal mode of address.

'I don't know, my dear. Your papa has sometimes talked of a house in town, or we might be abroad. I can only say that if we are at home here, we shall be very much pleased to see Miss Crofton again.'

I thanked her, kissed Milly once more, and so departed—to be driven to the station in state in the barouche, and to look sadly back at the noble old house in which I had been so happy.

Once more I returned to the dryasdust routine of Albury Lodge, and rang the changes upon history and geography, chronology and English grammar, physical science and the elements of botany, until my weary head ached and my heart grew sick. And when I came to be a governess, it would of course be the same thing over and over again, on a smaller scale. And this was to be my future, without hope of change or respite, until I grew an old woman worn-out with the drudgery of tuition!

CHAPTER V.

MILLY'S LETTER.

THE half-year wore itself slowly away. There were no incidents to mark the time, no change except the slow changes of the seasons; and my only pleasures were letters from home or from Emily Darrell.

Of the home letters I will not speak—they could have no interest except for myself; but Milly's are links in the story of a life. She wrote to me as freely as she had talked to me, pouring out all her thoughts and fancies with that confiding frankness which was one of the most charming attributes of her mind. For some time the letters contained nothing that could be called news; but late in September there came one which seemed to me to convey intelligence of some importance.

'You will be grieved to hear, my darling Mary,' she wrote, after a little playful discussion of my own affairs, 'that my stepmother and I are no nearer anything like a real friendship than we were when you left us. What it is that makes the gulf between us, I cannot tell; but there is something, some hidden feeling in both our minds, I think, which prevents our growing fond of each other. She is very kind to me, so far as perfect non interference with my doings, and a gracious manner when we are together, can go; but I am sure she does not like me. I have surprised her more than once looking at me with the strangest expression — a calculating, intensely thoughtful look, that made her face ten years older than it is at other times. Of course there are times when we are thrown together alone—though this does not occur often, for she and my father are a most devoted couple, and spend the greater part of every day together—and I have noticed at those times that she never speaks of her girlhood, or of any part of her life before her marriage. All that came before seems a blank page, or a sealed volume that she does not care to open. I asked some trifling question about her father once, and she turned upon me almost angrily.

"I do not care to speak about him, Milly," she said; "he was not a good father, and he is best forgotten. I never had a real friend till I met my husband."

'There is one part of her character which I am bound to appreciate. I believe that she is really grateful and devoted to papa, and he certainly seems thoroughly happy in her society. The marriage had the effect which I felt sure it must have — it has divided us two most completely; but if it has made him happy, I have no reason to complain. What could I wish for beyond his happiness?

'And now, Milly, for my news. Julian Stormont has been here, and has asked me to be his wife.

'He came over last Saturday afternoon, intending to stop with us till Monday morning. It was a bright warm day here, and in the afternoon he persuaded me to walk to Cumber Church with him. You remember the way we drove through the wood the day we went to the Priory, I daresay; but there is a nearer way than that for foot passengers, and I think a prettier one — a kind of cross-cut through the same wood. I consented willingly enough, having nothing better to do with myself, and we had a pleasant walk to church, talking of all kinds of things. As we returned Julian grew very serious, and when we were about half way upon our journey, he asked me if I could guess what had brought him over to Thornleigh. Of course I told him that I concluded

F

he had come as he usually did—for rest and change after the cares of business, and to talk about business affairs with papa.

'He told me he had come for something more than that. He came to tell me that he had loved me all his life; that there was nothing my father would like better than our union if it could secure my happiness, as he hoped and believed it might.

'I think you know, Mary, that no idea of this kind had ever entered my mind. I told Julian this, and told him that, however I might esteem him as my cousin, he could never be nearer or dearer to me than that. The change in his face when he heard this almost frightened me. He grew deadly pale, but I am certain it was anger rather than disappointment that was uppermost in his mind. I never knew until then what a hard cruel face it could be.

"Is this irrevocable, Emily?" he asked, in a cold firm voice; "is there no hope that you will change your mind by and by?"

"No, Julian; I am never likely to do that."

"There is some one else, then, I suppose," he said.

"No, indeed, there is no one else."

"Highly complimentary to me!" he cried, with a harsh laugh.

'I was very sorry for him, in spite of that angry look.

"Pray don't imagine that I do not appreciate your many high qualities, Julian," I said, "or that I do not feel honoured by your preference for me. No doubt there are many women in the world better deserving your regard than I am, who would be able to return it."

"Thank you for that little conventional speech," he cried with a sneer. "A man builds all his hopes of happiness on one woman, and she coolly shatters the fabric of his life, and then tells him to go and build elsewhere. I daresay there are women in the world who would condescend to marry me if I asked them, but it is my misfortune to care only for one woman. I can't transfer my affection, as a man transfers his capital from one form of investment to another."

'We walked on for some time in silence. I was determined not to be angry with him, however ungraciously he might speak to me; and when we were drawing near home, I begged that we might remain friends still, and that this unfortunate conversation might make no difference between us. I told him I knew how much my father valued him, and that it would distress me deeply if he deserted Thornleigh on my account.

"Friends!" he replied, in an absent tone; "yes, we are still friends of course, and I shall not desert Thornleigh."

'He seemed gayer than usual that evening after dinner. Whether the gaiety was assumed in order to hide his depression, or whether he was really able to take the matter lightly, I cannot tell. Of course I cannot shut out of my mind the consideration that a marriage with me would be a matter of great worldly advantage to Julian, who has nothing but the salary he receives from my father, and who by such a marriage would most likely secure immediate possession of the business, in which he is already a kind of deputy principal.

'I noticed that my stepmother was especially kind to Julian this evening, and that she and he sat apart in one of the windows for some time talking to each other in a low confidential tone, while my father took his after-dinner nap. I wonder whether he told her of our interview that afternoon?

'He went back to Shields early next morning, and bade me good-bye quite in his usual manner; so I hoped he had forgiven me; but the affair has left an unpleasant feeling in my mind, a sort of vague dread of some trouble to arise out of it in the future. I cannot forget that hard cruel look in my cousin's face.

'When he was gone, Mrs. Darrell began to praise him very warmly, and my father spoke of him in the same tone. They talked of him a good deal as we lingered over our breakfast, and I fancied there was some intention with regard to me in the minds of both—they seem indeed to think alike upon every subject. Dearly as I love my father, this is a point upon which even his influence could not affect me. I might be weak and yielding upon every other question, never upon this.

'And now let me tell you about my friend Peter, Rebecca Thatcher's half-witted grandson. You know how painfully we were both struck by the poor fellow's listless hopeless manner when we were at the cottage on the moor. I thought of it a great deal afterwards, and it occurred to me that our head-gardener might find work for him in the way of weeding, and rolling the gravel paths, and such humble matters. Brook is a good kind old man, and always ready to do anything to please me; so I asked him the question one day in August, and he promised that when he next wanted extra hands Peter Thatcher should be employed, "Though I don't suppose I shall ever make much of him, miss," he said; "but there's naught I wouldn't do to please you."

'Well, my dear Mary, the boy came, and has done so well as quite to surprise Brook and the other two gardeners. He has an extraordinary attachment to me, and nothing delights him so much as to wait upon me when I am attending to my ferns, a task I always perform myself, as you know. To see this poor boy, standing by with a watering-pot in one hand, and a little basket of dead leaves in the other, watching me as breathlessly as if I were some great surgeon operating upon a patient, would make you smile; but I think you could scarcely fail to be touched by his devotion. He tells me that he is so happy at Thornleigh, and he begins to look a great deal brighter already. The men say he is indefatigable in his work, and worth two ordinary boys. He is passionately fond of flowers, and I have begun to teach him the elements of botany. It is rather slow work impressing the names of the plants upon his poor feeble brain; but he is so anxious to learn, and so proud of being taught, that I am well repaid for my trouble.'

Milly was very anxious that I should spend Christmas at Thornleigh; but it was by that time nearly a year since I had seen the dear ones at home, and ill as my dear father could afford any addition to his expenses, he wished me to spend my holidays with him; and so it was arranged that I should return to Warwickshire, much to my dear girl's regret.

The holiday was a very happy one; and, before it was over, I received a letter from Milly, telling me that Mr. and Mrs. Darrell were going abroad for some months, and asking me to cut short my term at Albury Lodge, and come to Thornleigh as her companion, at a salary which I thought a very handsome one.

The idea of exchanging the dull monotony of Miss Bagshot's establishment for such a home as Thornleigh, with the friend I loved as dearly as a sister, was more than delightful to me, to say nothing of a salary which would enable me to buy my own clothes and leave a margin for an annual remittance to my father. I talked the subject over with him, and he wrote immediately to Miss Bagshot, requesting her to waive the half-year's notice of the withdrawal of my services, to which she was fairly entitled. This she consented very kindly to do; and instead of going back to Albury Lodge, I went to Thornleigh.

Mr. and Mrs. Darrell had started for Paris when I arrived, and the house seemed very empty and quiet. My dear girl came into the hall to receive me, and led me off to her pretty sitting-room, where there was a bright fire, and where, she told me, she spent almost the whole of her time now.

'And are you really pleased to come to me, Mary?' she asked, when our first greetings were over.

'More than pleased, my darling. It seems almost too bright a life for me. I can hardly believe in it yet.'

'But perhaps you will soon get as tired of Thornleigh as ever you did of Albury Lodge. It will be rather a dull kind of life, you know; only you and I and the old servants.'

'I shall never feel dull with you, Milly. But tell me how all this came about. How was it you didn't go abroad with Mr. and Mrs. Darrell?'

'Ah, that is rather strange, isn't it? The truth of the matter is, that Augusta did not want me to go with them. She does not like me, Mary, that is the real truth, though she affects to be very fond of me, and has contrived to make my father think she is so.

What is there that she cannot make him think? She does not like me; and she is never quite happy or at her ease when I am with her. She had been growing tired of Thornleigh for some time when the winter began; and she looked so pale and ill, that my father got anxious about her. The doctor here treated her in the usual stereotyped way, and made very light of her ailments, but recommended change of air and scene. Papa proposed going to Scarborough; but somehow or other Augusta contrived to change Scarborough into Paris, and they are to spend the winter and spring there, and perhaps go on to Germany in the summer. At first papa was very anxious to take me with them; but Augusta dropped some little hints—it would interrupt my studies, and unsettle me, and so on. You know I am rather proud, Mary, so you can imagine I was not slow to understand her. I said I would much prefer to stay at Thornleigh, and proposed immediately that you should come to me and be my companion, and help me on with my studies.'

'My dearest, how good of you to wish that!'

'It was not at all good. I think you are the only person in the world who really cares for me, now that I have lost papa—for I have lost him, you see, Mary;

that becomes more obvious every day. Well, dear, I had a hard battle to fight. Mrs. Darrell said you were absurdly young for such a position, and that I required a matronly person, able to direct and protect me, and take the management of the house in her absence, and so on; but I said that I wanted neither direction nor protection; that the house wanted no other management than that of Mrs. Bunce the housekeeper, who has managed it ever since I was a baby; and that if I could not have Mary Crofton, I would have no one at all. I told papa what an indefatigable darling you were, and how conscientiously you would perform anything you promised to do. So, after a good deal of discussion, the matter was settled; and here we are, with the house all to ourselves, and the prospect of being alone together for six months to come.'

I asked her if she had seen much of Mr. Stormont since that memorable Sunday afternoon.

'He has been here twice,' she said, 'for his usual short visit from Saturday afternoon till Monday morning, and he has treated me just as if that uncomfortable interview had never taken place.'

We were very happy together in the great lonely house, amongst old servants, who seemed to take a pleasure in waiting on us. We spent our mornings and evenings in Milly's sitting-room, and took our meals in a snug prettily-furnished breakfast-room on the ground-floor. We read together a great deal, going through a systematic course of study of a very different kind from the dry labours at Albury Lodge. There was a fine old library at Thornleigh, and we read the masters of English and French prose together with unflagging interest and pleasure. Besides all this, Milly worked hard at her music, and still harder at her painting, which was a real delight to her.

Mr. Collingwood the rector, and his family, came to see us, and insisted on our visiting them frequently in a pleasant unceremonious manner; and we had other invitations from Milly's old friends in the neighbourhood of Thornleigh.

There were carriages at our disposal, but we did not often use them. Milly preferred walking; and we used to take long rambles together whenever the weather was favourable—rambles across the moor, or far away over the hills, or deep into the wood between Thornleigh and Cumber.

CHAPTER VI.

A NEW ACQUAINTANCE.

IT was shortly after my arrival at Thornleigh that I first saw the man whose story I had heard in the study at Cumber Priory. Milly and I had been together about a fortnight, and it was the end of January—cold, clear, bright weather—when we set out early one afternoon for a ramble in our favourite wood, Milly furnished with pencils and sketch-book, in order to jot down any striking effect of the gaunt leafless old trees. She had a hardy disregard of cold in her devotion to her art, and would sit down to sketch in the bitter January weather in spite of my entreaties.

We stayed out longer than usual, and Milly had stopped once or twice to make a hasty sketch, when the sky grew suddenly dark, and big drops of rain began to fall slowly. These were speedily succeeded by a pelting storm of rain and hail, and we felt that we were caught, and must be drenched to the skin before we could get back to Thornleigh. The weather had been temptingly fine when we left home, and we had neither umbrellas nor any other kind of protection against the rain.

'We had better scamper off as fast as we can,' said Milly.

'But we can't run four miles. Hadn't we better go on to Cumber, and wait in the village till the weather changes, or try to get some kind of conveyance there?'

'Well, I suppose that would be best. There must be such a thing as a fly at Cumber, I should think, small as the place is. But it's nearly a mile from here to the village.'

'Anything seems better than going back through the wood in such weather,' I said.

We were close to the outskirts of the wood at this time, and within a very short distance of the Priory gates. While we were still pausing in an undecided way, with the rain pelting down upon us, a figure came towards us from among the leafless trees—the figure of a man, a gentleman, as we could see by his dress and bearing, and a stranger. We had never met any one but country-people, farm-labourers, and so on, in the wood before, and were a little startled by this apparition.

He came up to us quickly, lifting his hat as he approached us.

'Caught in the storm, ladies,' he said, 'and without umbrellas I see, too. Have you far to go?'

'Yes, we have to go as far as Thornleigh,' Milly answered.

'Quite impossible in such weather. Will you come into the Priory and wait till the storm is over?'

'The Priory! To be sure!' cried Milly. 'I never thought of that. I know the housekeeper very well, and I am sure she would let us stop there.'

We walked towards the Priory gates, the stranger accompanying us. I had no opportunity of looking at him under that pelting rain, but I was wondering all the time who he was, and how he came to speak of Cumber Priory in that familiar tone.

One of the gates stood open, and we went in.

'A desolate-looking place, isn't it?' said the stranger. 'Dismal enough, without the embellishment of such weather as this.'

He led the way to the hall-door, and opened it unceremoniously, standing aside for us to pass in before him. There was a fire burning in the wide old-fashioned fireplace, and the place had an air of occupation that was new to it.

'I'll send for Mrs. Mills, and she shall take your wet shawls away to be dried,' said the stranger, ringing a bell; and I think we both began to understand by this time that he must be the master of the house.

'You are very kind,' Milly answered, taking off her dripping shawl. 'I did not know that the Priory was occupied except by the old servants. I fear you must have thought me very impertinent just now when I talked so coolly of taking shelter here.'

'I am only too glad that you should find refuge in the old place.'

He wheeled a couple of ponderous carved-oak chairs close to the hearth, and begged us to sit there; but Milly preferred standing in the noble old gothic window looking out at the rain.

'They will be getting anxious about us at home,' she said, 'if we are not back before dark.'

'I wish I possessed a close carriage to place at your service. I do, indeed, boast of the ownership of a dog-cart, if you would not be afraid of driving in such a barbarous vehicle when the rain is over. It would keep you out of the mud, at any rate.'

Milly laughed gaily.

'I have been brought up in the country,' she said, 'and am not at all afraid of driving in a dog-cart. I used often to go out with papa in his, before he married.'

'Then, when the storm is over, I shall have the pleasure of driving you to Thornleigh, if you will permit me that honour.'

Milly looked a little perplexed at this, and made some excuse about not wishing to cause so much trouble.

'I really think we could walk home very well; don't you, Mary?' she said; and I declared myself quite equal to the walk.

'It would be impossible for you to get back to Thornleigh before dark,' the gentleman remonstrated. 'I shall be quite offended if you refuse the use of my dog-cart, and insist on getting wet feet. I daresay your feet are wet as it is, by the bye.'

We assured him of the thickness of our boots, and gave our shawls to Mrs. Mills the old housekeeper, who carried them off to be dried in the kitchen, and promised to convey the order about the dog-cart to the stables immediately.

I had time now to look at our new acquaintance, who was standing with his shoulders against one angle of the high oak mantelpiece, watching the rain beating against a window opposite to him. I had no difficulty in recognising the original of that portrait which Augusta Darrell had looked at so strangely. He was much older than when the portrait had been taken—ten years at the least, I thought. In the picture he looked little more than twenty, and I should have guessed him now to be on the wrong side of thirty.

He was handsome still, but the dark powerful face had a sort of rugged look, the heavy eyebrows overshadowed the sombre black eyes, a thick fierce-looking moustache shrouded the mouth, but could not quite conceal an expression, half cynical, half melancholy, that lurked about the lowered corners of the full firm lips. He looked like a man whose past life held some sad or sinful history.

I could fancy, as I looked at him, that last bitter interview with his mother, and I could imagine how hard and cruel such a man might be under the influence of an unpardonable wrong. Like Mrs. Darrell, I was inclined to place myself on the side of the unfortunate lovers, rather than on that of the mother, who had been willing to sacrifice her son's happiness to her pride of race.

We all three remained silent for some little time, Milly and I standing together in the window, Mr. Egerton leaning against the mantelpiece, watching the rain with an absent look in his face. He roused himself at last, as if with an effort, and came over to the window by which we stood.

'It looks rather hopeless at present,' he said; 'but I shall spin you over to Thornleigh in no time; so you mustn't be anxious. It is at Thornleigh Manor you live, is it not?'

'Yes,' Milly answered. 'My name is Darrell, and this young lady is Miss Crofton, my very dear friend.'

He bowed in recognition of this introduction.

'I thought as much—I mean as to your name being Darrell. I had the honour to know Mr. Darrell very well when I was a lad, and I have a vague recollection of a small child in a white frock, who, I think, must have been yourself. I have only been home a week, or I should have done myself the pleasure of calling on your father.'

'Papa is in Paris,' Milly answered, 'with my stepmother.'

'Ah, he has married again, I hear. One of the many changes that have come to pass since I was last in Yorkshire.'

'Have you returned for good, Mr. Egerton?'

'For good—or for evil—who knows?' he answered, with a careless laugh. 'As to whether I stay here so many weeks or so many years, that is a matter of supreme uncertainty. I never am in the same mind very long together. But I am heartily sick of knocking about abroad, and I cannot possibly find life emptier or duller here than I have found it in places that people call gay.'

'I can't fancy any one growing tired of such a place as the Priory,' said Milly.

'"Stone walls do not a prison make, nor iron bars a cage." "'Tis in ourselves that we are thus or thus." Cannot you fancy a man getting utterly tired of himself and his own thoughts—knowing himself by heart, and finding the lesson a dreary one? Perhaps not. A girl's life seems all brightness. What should such happy young creatures know of that arid waste of years that lies beyond a man's thirtieth birthday, when his youth has not been a fortunate one? Ah, there is a break in the sky yonder; the rain will be over presently.'

The rain did cease, as he had prophesied. The dog-cart was brought round to the door by a clumsy-looking man in corduroy, who seemed half groom, half gardener; and Mr. Egerton drove us home; Milly sitting next him, I at the back. His horse was a very good one, and the drive only lasted a quarter of an hour, during which time our new acquaintance talked very pleasantly to both of us.

I could not forget that Mr. Darrell had called him a bad man; but in spite of that sweeping condemnation I could not bring myself to think of him without a certain interest.

Of course Milly and I discussed Mr. Egerton as we sat over our snug little *tête-à-tête* dinner, and we were both inclined to speak of his blighted life in a pitying kind of way, and to blame his mother's conduct, little as we knew of the details of the story. Our existences were so quiet that this little incident made quite an event, and we were apt to date things from that afternoon for some time afterwards.

CHAPTER VII.

A LITTLE MATCH-MAKING.

WE heard nothing of Mr. Egerton for about three weeks, at the end of which time we were invited to dine at the Rectory. The first person we saw on going into the long, low, old-fashioned drawing-room was the master of Cumber Priory leaning against the mantelpiece in his favourite attitude. The Rector was not in the room when we arrived, and Angus Egerton was talking to Mrs. Collingwood, who sat in a low chair near the fire.

'Mr. Egerton has been telling me about your adventure in the wood, Milly,' Mrs. Collingwood said, as she rose to receive us. 'I hope it will be a warning to you to be more careful in future. I think that Cumber Wood is altogether too dangerous a place for two young ladies like you and Miss Crofton.'

'The safest place in the world,' cried Angus Egerton. 'I shall always be at hand to come to the ladies' assistance, and shall pray for the timely appearance of an infuriated bull, in order that I may distinguish myself by something novel in the way of a rescue. I hear that you are a very charming artist, Miss Darrell, and that you have done some of our oaks and beeches the honour to immortalise them.'

There is no need for me to record all the airy empty talk of that evening. It was a very pleasant evening. Angus Egerton had received his first lessons in the classics from the kind old Rector, and had been almost a son of the house in the past, the girls told me. He had resumed his old place upon his return, and seemed really fond of these friends, whom he had found ready to welcome him warmly in spite of all rumours to his disadvantage that had floated to Thornleigh during the years of his absence.

He was very clever, and seemed to have been everywhere, and to have seen everything worth seeing that the world contained. He had read a great deal too, in spite of his wandering life; and the fruit of his reading cropped up pleasantly now and then in his conversation.

There were no other guests, except an old country

squire, who talked of nothing but his farming. Milly sat next Angus Egerton ; and from my place on the other side of the table I could see how much she was interested in his talk. He did not stop long in the dining-room after we had left, but joined us as we sat round the fire in the drawing-room, talking over the poor people with Mrs. Collingwood and her two daughters, who were great authorities upon the question, and held a Dorcas society once a week, of which Milly and I were members.

There was the usual music—a little playing and a little singing from the younger ladies of the company, myself included. Milly sang an English ballad very sweetly, and Angus Egerton stood by the piano looking down at her while she sang.

Did he fall in love with her upon this first happy evening that those two spent together? I cannot tell ; but it is certain that after that evening he seemed to haunt us in our walks, and, go where we would, we were always meeting him, in company with a Scottish deerhound called Nestor, of which Milly became very fond. When we met in this half-accidental way he used to join us in our walk for a mile or two, very often bearing us company till we were within a few paces of Thornleigh.

These meetings, utterly accidental as they always were on our side, were a source of some perplexity to me. I was not quite certain whether I was right in sanctioning so close an acquaintance between Emily Darrell and the master of Cumber Priory. I knew that her father thought badly of him. Yet, what could I do? I was not old enough to pretend to any authority over my darling, nor had her father invested me with any; and I knew that her noble nature was worthy of all confidence. Beyond this, I liked Angus Egerton, and was inclined to trust him. So the time slipped away very pleasantly for all of us, and the friendship among us all three became closer day by day.

We met Mr. Egerton very often at the Rectory, and sometimes at other houses where we visited. He was much liked by the Thornleigh people, who had, most of them, known him in his boyhood; and it was considered by his old friends, that, whatever his career abroad might have been, he had begun, and was steadily pursuing, a reformed course of life. His means did not enable him to do much, but he was doing a little towards the improvement of Cumber Priory; and his existence there was as simple as that of the Master of Ravenswood.

I had noticed that Mrs. Collingwood did all in her power to encourage the friendship between Milly and Mr. Egerton, and one day in the spring, after they had met a great many times at her house, she spoke to me of her hopes quite openly.

It was a bright afternoon, and we were all strolling in the garden, after a game of croquet—the Rector's wife and I side by side, Milly and Angus a little way in front of us.

'I think she likes him,' Mrs. Collingwood said thoughtfully.

'Everybody seems to like Mr. Egerton,' I answered.

'O yes, I know that; but I mean something more than the ordinary liking. I am so anxious that he should marry—and marry wisely. I think I am almost as fond of him as if he were my son; and I should be so pleased if I could be the means of bringing about a match between them. Milly is just the girl to make a man happy, and her fortune would restore Cumber Priory to all its old glory.'

Her fortune! The word jarred upon me. Was it her money, after all, that Angus Egerton was thinking of when he took such pains to pursue my darling?

'I should be sorry for her to marry any one who cared for her money,' I said.

'Of course, my dear Miss Crofton; and so should I be sorry to see her throw herself away upon any one with whom her money was a paramount consideration. But one cannot put these things quite out of the question. I know that Angus admired her very much the first day he saw her, and I fancy his admiration has grown into a warmer feeling since then. He has said nothing to me upon the subject, nor I to him; for you know how silent he always is about himself. But I cannot help wishing that such a thing might come to pass. He has one of the best names in the North Riding, and a first-rate position as the owner of Cumber Priory. He only wants money.'

I was too young and inexperienced to take a worldly view of things, and from this moment felt disposed to distrust Mr. Egerton. I remembered the story of his early attachment, and told myself that a man who had loved once like that had in all probability worn out his powers of loving.

'I don't think Mr. Darrell would approve of, or even permit, such a marriage,' I said presently. 'I know he has a very bad opinion of Mr. Egerton.'

' On what account?'

' On account of his conduct to his mother.'

' No one knows the secret of that affair except Angus himself,' answered Mrs. Collingwood. ' I don't think any one has a right to think badly of him upon that ground. I knew Mrs. Egerton very well. She was a proud hard woman, capable of almost anything in order to accomplish any set purpose of her own. Up to the time when he went to Oxford Angus had been an excellent son.'

' Was it at Oxford he met the girl he wanted to marry?'

' No; it was somewhere in the west of England, where he went on a walking tour during the long vacation.'

' He must have loved her very much, to act as he did. I should doubt his power ever to love any one else.'

' That is quite a girl's way of thinking, my dear Miss Crofton. Depend upon it, after that kind of stormy first love, there generally comes a better and truer feeling. Angus was little more than a boy then. He is in the prime of manhood now, able to judge wisely, and not easily to be caught, or he would have married in all those years abroad.'

This seemed reasonable enough; but I was vexed, nevertheless, by Mrs. Collingwood's match-making notions, which seemed to disturb the peaceful progress of our lives. After this I looked upon every invitation to the Rectory—where we never went without meeting Mr. Egerton—as a kind of snare; but our visits there were always very pleasant, and I grew in time to think with more indulgence of the Rector's wife's desire for her favourite's advantage.

In all this time Angus Egerton had in no manner betrayed the state of his feelings. If he met us in our walks oftener than seemed possible by mere chance, there was nothing strictly lover-like in his tone or conduct. But I have seen his face light up as he met my dear girl at these times, and I have noticed a certain softening of his voice as he talked to her, that I never heard on other occasions.

And she? About her feelings I had much less doubt. She tried her uttermost to hide the truth from me, ashamed of her regard for one who had never yet professed to be more than a friend; but I knew that she loved him. It was impossible, in the perfect companionship and confidence of our lives, for Milly to keep this first secret of her pure young heart hidden from me. I knew that she loved him;

and I began to look forward anxiously to Mr. Darrell's return, which would relieve me of all responsibility, and perhaps put an end to our friendship with Angus Egerton.

CHAPTER VIII.

ON THE WATCH.

THE travellers came back to Thornleigh Manor in August, when the days were breathless and sultry, and the freshness of the foliage had already begun to fade after an unusually dry summer. Milly and I had been very happy together, and I think we both looked forward with a vague dread to the coming break in our lives. She loved her father as dearly as she had ever done, and longed ardently to see him again; but she knew as well as I did that our independence must end with his return.

'If he were coming back alone, Mary,' she said—'if that marriage were all a dream, and he were coming back alone—how happy I should be! I know that of his own free will he would never come between me and any wish of mine. But I don't know how he would act under his wife's influence. You cannot imagine the power she has over him. And we shall have to begin the old false life over again, she and I—disliking and distrusting each other in our hearts—the daily round of civilities and ceremonies and pretences. O Mary, you cannot think how I hate it.'

We had seen nothing of Julian Stormont during all the time of our happy solitude; but on the day appointed for Mr. and Mrs. Darrell's return he came to Thornleigh, looking more careworn than ever. I pitied him a little, knowing the state of his feelings about Milly, believing indeed that he loved her with a rare intensity, and being inclined to attribute the change in him to his disappointment upon this subject.

Milly told him how ill he was looking, and he said something about hard work and late hours, with a little bitter laugh.

'It doesn't matter to any one whether I am well or ill, you see, Milly,' he said. 'What would any one care if I were to drop over the side of the quay some dark night, on my way from the office to my lodgings, after a hard day's work, and never be seen alive again?'

'How wicked it is of you to talk like that, Julian! There are plenty of people who would care—papa, to begin with.'

'Well, I suppose my uncle William would be rather sorry. He would lose a good man of business, and he would scarcely like going back to the counting-house, and giving himself up to all the dry details of commerce once more.'

The travellers arrived soon after this. Mr. Darrell greeted his daughter with much tenderness; but I noticed a kind of languor in Mrs. Darrell's embrace, very different from her reception of Milly at that first meeting which I had witnessed more than a year before. It seemed to me that her power over her husband was now supreme, and that she did not trouble herself to keep up any pretence of affection for his only child.

She was dressed to perfection; and that subdued charm which was scarcely beauty, and yet stood in place of it, attracted me to-day as it had done when we first met. She was a woman who, I could imagine, might be more admired than many handsomer women. There was a distinction, an originality about the pale delicate face, dark arched brows, and gray eyes—eyes which were at times very brilliant.

She looked round her without the faintest show of interest or admiration as she loitered with her husband on the terrace, while innumerable travelling-bags, shawls, books, newspapers, and packages were being carried from the barouche to the house.

'How dry and burnt-up everything looks!' she said.

'Have you no better greeting than that for Thornleigh, my dear Augusta?' Mr. Darrell asked in rather a wounded tone. 'I thought you would be pleased to see the old place again.'

'Thornleigh Manor is not a passion of mine,' she answered. 'I hope you will take a house in town at the beginning of next year.'

She passed on into the hall, after having honoured me with the coldest possible shake-hands. We saw no more of her until nearly dinner-time, when she came down to the drawing-room, dressed in white, and looking deliciously pale and cool in the sultry weather. Milly had spent the afternoon in going round the gardens and home-farm with her father, and had thoroughly enjoyed the delight of a couple of hours alone with him. She gave him up now to Mrs. Darrell, who devoted all her attention to him for the rest of the evening; while Julian Stormont, Milly, and I loitered about the garden, and played a desultory game of croquet.

It was not until the next morning that Mr. Egerton's name was mentioned, although it had been in my thoughts, and I cannot doubt in Milly's, ever since Mr. Darrell's arrival. We were in the drawing-room after breakfast, not quite decided what to do with the day, when Mr. Darrell came into the room dressed for a ride with his wife. He went over to the window by which Milly was standing.

'You have quite given up riding, Ellis tells me, my dear,' he said.

'I have not cared to ride while you were away, papa, as Mary does not ride.'

'Miss Crofton might have learnt to ride; there would always be a horse at her disposal.'

'We like walking better,' Milly said, blushing a little, and fidgeting nervously with one of the buttons on her father's coat. 'I used to feel in the way, you know, when I rode with you and Mrs. Darrell.'

'That was your own fault, Milly,' he answered, with a displeased look.

'I suppose it was. But I think Augusta felt it too. O, by the bye, papa, I did not tell you quite all the news when we were out together yesterday.'

'Indeed!'

'No; I forgot to mention that Mr. Egerton has come back.'

'Angus Egerton?'

'Yes; he came back last winter.'

'You never said so in your letters.'

'Didn't I? I suppose that was because I knew you were rather prejudiced against him; and one can't explain away that kind of thing in a letter.'

'You would find it very difficult to explain away my dislike of Angus Egerton, either in or out of a letter. Have you seen much of him?'

'A good deal. He has been at the Rectory very often when Mary and I have been invited there. The Collingwoods are very fond of him. I am sure—I think—you will like him, papa, when you come to see a little of him. He is going to call upon you.'

'He can come if he pleases,' Mr. Darrell answered with an indifferent air; 'I shall not be uncivil to him. But I am rather sorry that he has made such a favourable impression upon you, Milly.'

She was still playing with the buttons of his coat, looking downward, her dark eyes quite veiled by their long lashes.

'I did not say that, papa,' she murmured shyly.

'But I am sure of it from your manner. Has he done anything towards the improvement of Cumber?'

'O yes; he has put new roofs to some part of the

stables; and the land is in better order, they say; and the gardens are kept nicely now.'

'Does he live alone at the Priory?'

'Quite alone, papa.'

'He must find it rather a dull business, I should think.'

'Mr. Collingwood says he is very fond of study, and that he has a wonderful collection of old books. He is a great smoker too, I believe; he walks a good deal; and he hunted all last winter. They say he is a tremendous rider.'

Augusta Darrell came in at this moment, ready for her ride. Her slim willowy figure looked to great advantage in the plain tight-fitting cloth habit; and the little felt hat with its bright scarlet feather gave a coquettish expression to her face. She tapped her husband lightly on the arm with her riding-whip.

'Now, William, if you are quite ready.'

'My dearest, I have been waiting for the last half-hour.'

They went off to their horses. Milly followed them to the terrace, and watched them as they rode away.

We spent the morning out-of-doors sketching,

with Julian Stormont in attendance upon us. At two o'clock we all met at luncheon.

After luncheon Milly and I went to the drawing-room, while Mrs. Darrell and Mr. Stormont strolled out upon the terrace. My dear girl had a sort of restless manner to-day, and went from one occupation to another, now sitting for a few minutes at the piano, playing brief snatches of pensive melody, now taking up a book, only to throw it down again with a little weary sigh. She seated herself at a table presently, and began to arrange the sketches in her portfolio. While she was doing this a servant announced Mr. Egerton. She rose hurriedly, blushing as I had rarely seen her blush before, and looking towards the open window near her, almost as if she would have liked to make her escape from the room. It was the first time Angus Egerton had been at Thornleigh Manor since she was a little child.

'Tell papa that Mr. Egerton is here, Filby,' she said to the servant. 'I think you will find him in the library.'

She had recovered her self-possession in some measure by the time she came forward to shake hands with the visitor; and in a few minutes we were talking in the usual easy friendly way.

'You see, I have lost no time in calling upon your papa, Miss Darrell,' he said presently. 'I am not too proud to show him how anxious I am to regain his friendship, if, indeed, I ever possessed it.'

Mr. Darrell came into the room as he was speaking; and however coldly he might have intended to receive the master of Cumber Priory, his manner soon softened and grew more cordial. There was a certain kind of charm about Angus Egerton, not very easily to be described, which I think had a potent influence upon all who knew him.

I fancied that Mr. Darrell felt this, and struggled against it, and ended by giving way to it. I saw that he watched his daughter closely, even anxiously, when she was talking to Angus Egerton, as if he had already some suspicion about the state of her feelings with regard to him. Mr. Egerton had caught sight of the open portfolio, and had insisted on looking over the sketches—not the first of Milly's that he had seen by a great many. I noticed the grave, almost tender, smile with which he looked at the little artistic 'bits' out of Cumber Wood. He went on talking to Mr. Darrell all the time he was looking at these sketches; talking of the neighbourhood and the changes that had come about of late years, and a little of the

Priory, and his intentions with regard to improvements.

'I can only creep along at a snail's pace,' he said; 'for I am determined not to get into debt, and I won't sell.'

'I wonder you never tried to let the Priory in all those years that you were abroad,' suggested Mr. Darrell.

Mr. Egerton shook his head, with a smile.

'I couldn't bring myself to that,' he said, 'though I wanted money badly enough. There has never been a strange master at Cumber since it belonged to the Egertons. I daresay it's a foolish piece of sentimentality on my part; but I had rather fancy the old place rotting slowly to decay than in the occupation of strangers.'

He was standing by the table where the open portfolio lay, with Milly by his side, and one of the sketches in his hands, when Mrs. Darrell came in at the window nearest to this little group, and stood on the threshold looking at him. I think I was the only person who saw her face at that moment. It was so sudden a look that came upon it, a look half terror, half pain, and it passed away so quickly, that I had scarcely time to distinguish the expression before it was gone; but it was a look that brought back to my memory the almost forgotten scene in the little study at Cumber Priory, and set me wondering what it could be that made the sight of Angus Egerton, either on canvas or in the flesh, a cause of agitation to Milly's stepmother.

In the next moment Mr. Darrell was presenting his visitor to his wife; and as the two acknowledged the introduction, I stole a glance at Mr. Egerton's face. It was paler than usual; and the expression of Mrs. Darrell's countenance seemed in a manner reflected in it. It was not possible that such looks could be without some significance. I felt convinced that these two people had met before.

There was a change in Mr. Egerton's manner from the moment of that introduction. He laid down Milly's sketch without another word, and stood with his eyes fixed on Augusta Darrell's face with a strange half-bewildered look, like a man who doubts the evidence of his own senses. Mrs. Darrell, on the contrary, seemed, after that one look which I had seen, quite at her ease, and rattled on gaily about the delight of travelling in the Tyrol, as compared to the dulness of life at Thornleigh.

'I hope you will enliven us a little, Mr. Egerton,'

she said. 'It is quite an agreeable surprise to find a new neighbour.'

'I ought to be very much flattered by that remark; but I doubt my power to add to the liveliness of this part of the world. And I do not think I shall stay much longer at Cumber.'

Milly glanced up at him with a surprised look.

'Mrs. Collingwood told us you were quite settled at the Priory,' she said, 'and that you intended to spend the rest of your days as a country squire.'

'I may have dreamed such a dream sometimes, Miss Darrell; but there are dreams that never fulfil themselves.'

He had recovered himself by this time, and spoke in his accustomed tone. Mr. Darrell asked him to dinner on an early day, when I knew the Rectory people were coming to us, and the invitation was accepted.

Julian Stormont had followed Mrs. Darrell in from the terrace, and had remained in the background, a very attentive listener and observer during the conversation that followed.

'So that is Angus Egerton,' he said, when our visitor had left us.

'Yes, Julian. O, by the bye, I forgot to introduce you; you came in so quietly,' answered Mr. Darrell.

'I can't say I particularly care about the honour of knowing that gentleman,' said Mr. Stormont in a half-contemptuous tone.

'Why not?' Milly asked quickly.

'Because I never heard any good of him.'

'But he has reformed, it seems,' said Mr. Darrell, 'and is leading quite a steady life at Cumber, the Collingwoods tell me. Augusta and I called at the Rectory this morning, and the Rector and his wife talked a good deal of him. I was rather pleased with him, I confess, just now.'

Milly looked up at her father gratefully. Poor child! how innocently and unconsciously she betrayed her secret! and how little she thought of the jealous eyes that were watching her! I saw Julian Stormont's face darken with an angry look, and I knew that he had already discovered the state of Milly's feelings in relation to Angus Egerton.

He was still with us when Mr. Egerton came to dinner two days later. I shall never forget that evening. The day was oppressively warm, with that dry sultry heat of which there had been so much during the latter part of the summer; and as the afternoon advanced, the air grew still, with that palpable stillness which so often comes before a thunder-storm. Milly had been full of life and vivacity all day, flitting from room to room with a kind of joyous restlessness. She took unusual pains with her toilette for so simple a party, and came into my room looking like Titania in her gauzy white dress, with half-blown blush-roses in her hair, and more roses in a bouquet at her waist.

Mr. Egerton came a little later than the party from the Rectory, and after shaking hands with Mr. Darrell, made his way at once to the place where Milly and I were sitting.

'Any more sketching since I was here last, Miss Darrell?' he asked.

'No. I have been doing nothing for the last day or two.'

'Do you know I have been thinking of your work in that way a good deal since I called here. I am stronger in criticism than in execution, you know. I think I was giving you a little lecture on your shortcomings, wasn't I?'

'Yes; but you left off so abruptly in the middle of it, that I don't fancy it was very profitable to me,' Milly answered in rather a piqued tone.

'Did I really? O yes, I remember. I was quite

startled by Mrs. Darrell's appearance. She is so surprisingly like a lady I knew a long time ago.'

'That is rather a curious coincidence,' I said.

'How a coincidence?' asked Mr. Egerton.

'Mrs. Darrell said almost the same thing about your portrait when we were at Cumber one day. It reminded her of some one she had known long ago.'

'What an excellent memory you have for small events, Miss Crofton!' said a voice close behind me. It was Mrs. Darrell's. She had come across the room towards us, unobserved by me, at any rate. Whether Angus Egerton had seen her or not, I do not know. He rose to shake hands with her, and then went on talking about Milly's sketching.

Mr. Collingwood took Mrs. Darrell in to dinner, and Mr. Egerton gave his arm to Milly, and was seated next her at the prettily decorated table, upon which there was always a wealth of roses at this time of year. I saw Augusta Darrell's eyes wander restlessly in that direction many times during dinner, and I felt that the dear girl I loved so fondly was in an atmosphere of falsehood. What was the nature of the past acquaintance between those two people? and why was it tacitly denied by both of them? If it had been an ordinary friendship, there could have been no reason for this concealment and suppression. I had never quite made up my mind to trust Angus Egerton, though I liked and admired him; and this mysterious relation between him and Augusta Darrell was a sufficient cause for serious distrust.

'I wish she cared for him less,' I said to myself, as I glanced at Milly's bright happy face.

When we went back to the drawing-room after dinner, the Miss Collingwoods had a great deal to say to Milly about a grand croquet-match which was to take place in a week or two at Pensildon, Sir John and Lady Pensildon's place, fourteen miles from Thornleigh. The Rector's daughters, both of whom were several years older than Milly, were passionately fond of croquet and everything in the way of gaiety, and were full of excitement about this coming event, discussing what they were going to wear, and what Milly was going to wear, on the occasion. While they were engaged in this way, Mrs. Collingwood told me a long story about one of her poor parishioners, always an inexhaustible subject with her. This arrangement left Mrs. Darrell unoccupied; and after standing at one of the open windows looking listlessly out, she sauntered out upon the terrace, her favourite lounge always in this summer weather. I saw her repass the windows a few minutes afterwards, in earnest conversation with Angus Egerton. This was some time before the other gentlemen left the dining-room; and they were still walking slowly up and down when Mr. Darrell and the Rector came to the drawing-room. The storm had not yet come, and it was bright moonlight. Mr. Darrell went out and brought his wife in, with some gentle reproof on her imprudence in remaining out of doors so late in her thin muslin dress.

After this there came some music. Augusta Darrell sang some old English ballads which I had never heard her sing before—simple pathetic melodies, which, I think, brought tears to the eyes of all of us.

Mr. Egerton sat near one of the open windows, with his face in shadow, while she was singing; and as she began the last of these old songs he rose with a half-impatient gesture, and went out upon the terrace. If I watched him closely, and others in relation to him, at this time, it was from no frivolous or impertinent curiosity, but because I felt very certain my darling's happiness was at stake. I saw her little disappointed look when he remained at the farther end of the room, talking to the gentlemen, all the rest of that evening, instead of contriving by some means to be near her, as he always had done during our pleasant evenings at the Rectory.

CHAPTER IX.

ANGUS EGERTON IS REJECTED.

THE expected storm came next day, and Milly and I were caught in it. We had gone for a ramble across the moor, and were luckily within a short distance of Rebecca Thatcher's cottage when the first vivid flash broke through the leaden clouds, and the first long peal of thunder came crashing over the open landscape. We set off for Mrs. Thatcher's habitation at a run, and arrived there breathless.

The herbalist was not alone. A tall dark figure stood between us and the little window as we went in, blotting out all the light.

Milly gave a faint cry of surprise; and as the figure turned towards us I recognised Mr. Egerton.

In all our visits among the poor we had never met him before.

'Caught again, young ladies!' he cried, laughing; 'you've neither of you grown weatherwise yet, I see. Luckily you're under cover before the rain has begun. I think we shall have it pretty heavy presently. How surprised you look to see me here, Miss Darrell! Becky is a very old friend of mine. I remember her ever since I can remember anything. She was in my grandfather's service once upon a time.'

'That I was, Mr. Egerton, and there's nothing I wouldn't do for you and yours—for you at least, for there's none but you left now. But I suppose you'll be getting married one of these days; you're not going to let the old name of Egerton die out?'

Angus Egerton shook his head with a slow sad gesture.

'I am too poor to marry, Mrs. Thatcher,' he said. 'What could I offer a wife but a gloomy old house, and a perpetual struggle to make hundreds do the work of thousands? I am too proud to ask the woman I love to sacrifice her future to me.'

'Cumber Priory is good enough for any woman that ever lived,' answered Rebecca Thatcher. 'You don't mean what you say, Mr. Egerton. You know that the name you bear is counted better than money in these parts.'

He laughed, and changed the conversation.

'I heard you young ladies talking a great deal of the Pensildon fête last night,' he said.

'Did you really?' asked Milly; 'you did not appear to be much interested in our conversation.'

'Did I seem distrait? It is a way I have sometimes, Miss Darrell; but I can assure you I can hear two or three conversations at once. I think I heard all that you and the Miss Collingwoods were saying.'

'You are going to Lady Pensildon's on the 31st, I suppose?' Milly said.

'I think not. I think of going abroad for the autumn. I have been rather a long time at Cumber, you know, and I'm afraid the roving mood is coming upon me again. I shall be sorry to go, too, for I had intended to torment you continually about your art studies. You have really a genius for landscape, you know, Miss Darrell; you only want to be goaded into industry now and then by some severe critic like myself. Is your cousin, Mr. Stormont, an artist, by the way?'

'Not at all.'

'That's a pity. He seems a clever young man. I suppose he will be a good deal with you, now that Mr. and Mrs. Darrell have returned?'

'He cannot stay very long at a time. He has the chief position in papa's counting-house.'

'Indeed! He looked a little as if the cares of business weighed upon his spirit.'

He glanced rather curiously at Milly while he was speaking of Mr. Stormont. Was he really going away, I wondered, or was that threat of departure only a lover-like ruse?

The rain came presently with all the violence usual to a thunder-shower. We were prisoners in Mrs. Thatcher's cottage for more than an hour; a happy hour, I think, to Milly, in spite of the closeness of the atmosphere and the medical odour of the herbs. Angus Egerton stood beside her chair all the time, looking down at her bright face and talking to her; while Mrs. Thatcher mumbled a long catalogue of her ailments and troubles into my somewhat inattentive ear.

Once while those two were talking about his intended departure I heard Mr. Egerton say,

'If I thought any one cared about my staying—if I could believe that any one would miss me ever so little—I should be in no hurry to leave Yorkshire.'

Of course Milly told him that there were many people who would miss him—Mr. Collingwood for instance, and all the family at the Rectory. He bent over her, and said something in a very low voice—something that brought vivid blushes to her face; and a few minutes afterwards they went to the door to look at the weather, and stood there talking till I had heard the last of Mrs. Thatcher's woes, and was free to join them. I had never seen Milly look so lovely as she did just then, with her downcast eyes, and a little tremulous smile upon her perfect mouth.

Mr. Egerton walked all the way home with us. The storm was quite over, the sun shining, and the air full of that cool freshness which comes after rain. We talked of all kinds of things. Mr. Egerton had almost made up his mind to spend the autumn at Cumber, he told us; and he would go to the Pensildon fête, and take Milly's side in the croquet-match. He seemed in almost boyish spirits during that homeward walk.

When we went up-stairs to our rooms that night, Milly followed me into mine. There was nothing new in this; we often wasted half an hour in happy idle talk before going to bed; but I was sure from my darling's manner she had something to tell me. She went over to an open window, and stood there with her face turned away from me, looking out across the distant moonlit sea.

'Mary,' she said, after a very long pause, 'do you think people are intended to be quite happy in this world?'

'My dear love, how can I answer such a question as that? I think that many people have their lives in their own hands, and that it rests with themselves to find happiness. And there are many natures that are elevated and purified by sorrow. I cannot tell what is best for us, dear. I cannot pretend to guess what this life was meant to be.'

'There is something in perfect happiness that frightens one, Mary. It seems as if it could not last. If it could, if I dared believe in it, I should think that my life was going to be quite happy.'

'Why should it be otherwise, my dear Milly? I don't think you have ever known much sorrow.'

'Not since my mother died—and I was only a child then—but that old pain has never quite gone out of my heart; and papa's marriage has been a greater grief to me than you would believe, Mary. This house has never seemed to be really my home since then. No, dear, it is a new life that is dawning for me—and O, such a bright one!'

She put her arms round my neck, and hid her face upon my shoulder.

'Can you guess what Angus Egerton said to me to-day?' she asked, in a low tremulous voice.

'Was it something very wonderful, dear — or something as old as the world we live in?'

'Not old to me, Mary — new and wonderful beyond all measure. I did not think he cared for me — I had never dared to hope; for I have liked him a little for a long time, dear, though I don't suppose you ever thought so.'

'My dear girl, I have known it from the very beginning. There is nothing in the world more transparent than your thoughts about Angus Egerton have been to me.'

'O Mary, how could you! And I have been so careful to say nothing!' she cried reproachfully. 'But he loves me, dear. He has loved me for a long time, he says; and he has asked me to be his wife.'

'What, after all those protestations about never asking a woman to share his poverty?'

'Yes, Mary; and he meant what he said. He told me that if I had been a penniless girl, he should have proposed to me ever so long ago. And he is to see papa to-morrow.'

'Do you think Mr. Darrell will ever consent to such a marriage, Milly?' I asked gravely.

'Why should he not? He cannot go on thinking badly of Angus when every one else thinks so well of him. You must have seen how he has softened towards him since they met. Mr. Egerton's old family and position are quite an equivalent for my money, whatever that may be. O Mary, I don't think papa can refuse his consent.'

'I am rather doubtful about that, Milly. It's one thing to like Mr. Egerton very well as a visitor — quite another to accept him as a son-in-law. Frankly, my dearest, I fear your father will be against the match.'

'Mary,' cried Milly reproachfully, 'I can see what it is—you are prejudiced against Mr. Egerton.'

'I am only anxious for your welfare, darling. I like Mr. Egerton very much. It is difficult for any one to avoid liking him. But I confess that I cannot bring myself to put entire trust in him.'

'Why not?'

I did not like to tell her the chief reason for my distrust — that mysterious relation between Angus Egerton and Mrs. Darrell. The subject was a serious—almost a dangerous—one; and I had no positive evidence to bring forward in proof of my fancy. It was a question of looks and words that had been full of significance to me, but which might seem to Milly to mean very little.

'We cannot help our instinctive doubts, dear. But if you can trust Mr. Egerton, and if your father can trust him, my fancies can matter very little. I cannot stand between you and your love, dear—I know that.'

'But you can make me very unhappy by your doubts, Mary,' she answered.

I kissed her, and did my best to console her; but she was not easily to be comforted, and left me in a half-sorrowful, half-angry mood. I had disappointed her, she told me—she had felt so sure of my sympathy; and instead of sharing her happiness, I had made her miserable by my fanciful doubts and gloomy forebodings. After she had gone, I sat by the window for a long time, thinking of her disconsolately, and feeling myself very guilty. But I had a fixed conviction that Mr. Darrell would refuse to receive Angus Egerton as his daughter's suitor, and that the course of this love-affair was not destined to be a smooth one.

The result proved that I had been right. Mr.

Egerton had a long interview with Mr. Darrell in the library next morning, during which his proposal was most firmly rejected. Milly and I knew that he was in the house, and my poor girl walked up and down our sitting-room with nervously clasped hands and an ashy pale face all the time those two were together down-stairs.

She turned to me with a little piteous look when she heard Angus Egerton ride away from the front of the house.

'O Mary, what is my fate to be?' she asked. 'I think he has been rejected. I do not think he would have gone away without seeing me if the interview had ended happily.'

A servant came to summon us both to the library. We went down together, Milly's cold hand clasped in mine.

Mr. Darrell was not alone. His wife was sitting with her back to the window, very pale, and with an angry brightness in her eyes.

'Sit down, Miss Crofton,' Mr. Darrell said very coldly; 'and you, Milly, come here.'

She went towards him with a slow faltering step, and sank down into the chair to which he pointed, looking at him all the time in an eager beseeching way that I think must have gone to his heart. He was standing with his back to the empty fireplace, and remained standing throughout the interview.

'I think you know that I love you, Milly,' he began, 'and that your happiness is the chief desire of my mind.'

'I am sure of that, papa.'

'And yet you have deceived me.'

'Deceived you? O papa, in what way?'

'By encouraging the hopes of a man whom you must have known I would never receive as your husband; by suffering your feelings to become engaged, without one word of warning to me, and in a manner that you must have known could not fail to be most obnoxious to me.'

'O papa, I did not know; it was only yesterday that Mr. Egerton spoke for the first time. There has been nothing hidden from you.'

'Nothing? Do you call your intimate acquaintance with this man nothing? He may have delayed any actual declaration until my return—with an artful appearance of consideration for me; but some kind of love-affair must have been going on between you all the time.'

'No, indeed, papa; until yesterday there was

never anything but the most ordinary acquaintance. Mary knows—'

'Pray don't appeal to Miss Crofton,' her father interrupted sternly. 'Miss Crofton has done very wrong in encouraging this affair. Miss Crofton heard my opinion of Angus Egerton a long time ago.'

'Mary has done nothing to encourage our acquaintance. It has been altogether a matter of accident from first to last. What have you said to Mr. Egerton, papa? Tell me at once, please.'

She said this with a quiet firmness, looking bravely up at him all the while.

'I have told him that nothing would induce me to consent to such a marriage. I have forbidden him ever to see you again.'

'That seems very hard, papa.'

'I thought you knew my opinion of Mr. Egerton.'

'It would change if you knew more of him.'

'Never. I might like him very well as a member of society; I could never approve of him as a son-in-law. Besides, I have other views for you—long-cherished views—which I hope you will not disappoint.'

'I don't know what you mean by that, papa; but I know that I can never marry any one except Mr. Egerton. I may never marry at all, if you refuse to change your decision upon this subject; but I am quite sure I shall never be the wife of any one else.'

Her father looked at her angrily. That hard expression about the lower part of the face, which I had noticed in his portrait and in himself from the very first, was intensified to-day. He looked a stern resolute man, whose will was not to be moved by a daughter's pleading.

'We shall see about that by and by,' he said. 'I am not going to have my plans defeated by a girl's folly. I have been a very indulgent father, but I am not a weak or yielding one. You will have to obey me, Milly, or you will find yourself a substantial sufferer by and by.'

'If you mean that you will disinherit me, papa, I am quite willing that you should do that,' Milly answered resolutely. 'Perhaps you think Mr. Egerton cares for my fortune. Put him to the test, papa. Tell him that you will give me nothing, and that he may take me on that condition.'

Augusta Darrell turned upon her stepdaughter

with a sudden look in her face that was almost like a flame.

'Do you think him so disinterested?' she asked.

'Have you such supreme confidence in his affection?'

'Perfect confidence.'

'And you do not believe that mercenary considerations have any weight with him? You do not think that he is eager to repair his shattered fortunes? You think him all truth and devotion? He, a *blasé* man of the world, of three-and-thirty; a man who has outlived the possibility of anything like a real attachment; a man who lavished his whole stock of feeling upon the one attachment of his youth.'

She said all this very quietly, but with a suppressed bitterness. I think it needed all her powers of restraint to keep her from some passionate outburst that would have betrayed the secret of her life. I was now more than ever convinced that she had known Angus Egerton in the past, and that she had loved him.

'You see, I am not afraid of his being put to the test,' Milly said proudly. 'I know that he loved some one very dearly, a long time ago. He spoke of that yesterday. He told me that his old love had died out of his heart years ago.'

'He told you a lie,' cried Mrs. Darrell. 'Such things never die. They sleep, perhaps—like the creatures that hide themselves in the ground and lie torpid all the winter—but with one breath of the past they flame into life again.'

'I am not going to make any such foolish trial of your lover's faith, Milly,' said Mr. Darrell. 'Whether your fortune is or is not a paramount consideration with him can make no possible difference in my decision. Nothing will ever induce me to consent to your marrying him. Of course, if you choose to defy me, you are of age and your own mistress; but on the day that makes you Angus Egerton's wife you will cease to be my daughter.'

'Papa,' cried Milly, 'you will break my heart.'

'Nonsense, child; hearts are not so easily broken. Let me hear no more of this unfortunate business. I have spoken to you very plainly, in order that there might be no chance of misunderstanding between us; and I rely upon your honour that there shall be no clandestine meeting between you and Angus Egerton in the future. I look to you, Miss Crofton, also, and shall hold you answerable for any accidental encounters out walking.'

'You need not be afraid, papa,' Milly answered

disconsolately. 'I daresay Mr. Egerton will leave Yorkshire, as he spoke of doing yesterday.'

'I hope he may,' said Mr. Darrell.

Milly rose to leave the room. Half-way towards the door she stopped, and turned her white despairing face towards her father with a hopeless look.

'I shall obey you, papa,' she said. 'I could not bear to forfeit your love, even for his sake. But I think you will break my heart.'

Mr. Darrell went over to her and kissed her.

'I am acting best for your ultimate happiness, Milly, be sure of that,' he said in a kinder tone than he had used before. 'There, my love, go and be happy with Miss Crofton, and let us all agree to forget this business as quickly as possible.'

This was our dismissal. We went back to Milly's pretty sitting-room, where the sun was shining and the warm summer air blowing on birds and flowers, and books and drawing materials, and all the airy trifles that had made our lives pleasant to us until that hour. Milly sat on a low stool at my feet, and buried her face in my lap, refusing all comfort. She sat like this for about an hour, weeping silently, and then rose suddenly and wiped the tears from her pale face.

'I am not going to lead you a miserable life about this, Mary,' she said. 'We will never speak of it after to-day. And I will try to do my duty to papa, and bear my life without that new happiness, which made it seem so bright. Do you think Mr. Egerton will feel the disappointment very much, Mary?'

'He cannot help feeling it, dear, if he loves you —as I believe he does.'

'And we might have been so happy together! I was dreaming of Cumber Priory all last night. I thought it had been restored with some of my money, and that the old house was full of life and brightness. Will he go away, do you think, Mary?'

'I should think it very likely.'

'And I shall never see him any more. I could not forfeit papa's love, Mary.'

'It would be a hard thing if you were to do that for the sake of a stranger, dear.'

'No, no, Mary; he is not a stranger to me; Angus Egerton is not a stranger. I know that he is noble and good. But my father was all the world to me a year ago. I could not do without his love. I must obey him.'

'Believe me, dear, it will be wisest and best to

do so. You cannot tell what changes may come to pass in the future. Obedience will make you very dear to your father; and the time may come in which he will think better of Mr. Egerton.'

'O Mary, if I could hope that!'

'Hope for everything, dear, if you do your duty.'

She grew a little more cheerful after this, and met her father at dinner with quite a placid face, though it was still very pale. Mrs. Darrell looked at her wonderingly, and with a half-contemptuous expression, I thought, as if this passion of her stepdaughter's seemed to her a very poor thing, after all.

Before the week was out, we heard that Mr. Egerton had left Yorkshire. We did not go to the Pensildon fête. Milly had a cold and kept her room, much to the regret of the Miss Collingwoods, who called every day to inquire about her. She made this cold—which was really a very slight affair—an excuse for a week's solitude, and at the end of that time reappeared among us with no trace of her secret sorrow. It was only I, who was always with her, and knew her to the core of her heart, who could have told how hard a blow that disappointment had been, and how much it cost her to bear it so quietly.

K

CHAPTER X.

CHANGES AT THORNLEIGH.

THE autumn and the early winter passed monotonously enough. There was a good deal of company at Thornleigh Manor at first, for Mrs. Darrell hated solitude; but after a little time she grew tired of the people her husband knew, and the dinners and garden parties became less frequent. I had found out, very soon after her return, that she was not happy—that this easy prosperous life was in some manner a burden to her. It was only in her husband's presence that she made any pretence of being pleased or interested in things. With him she was always the same—always deferential, affectionate, and attentive; while he, on his side, was the devoted slave of her every whim and wish.

She was not unkind to Milly, but those two seemed instinctively to avoid each other.

The winter brought trouble to Thornleigh Manor. It was well for Milly that she had tried to do her duty to her father, and had submitted herself patiently to his will. About a fortnight before Christmas Mr. Darrell went to North Shields to make his annual investigation of the wharves and warehouses, and to take a kind of review of the year's business. He never returned alive. He was seized with an apoplectic fit in the office, and carried to his hotel speechless. His wife and Milly were summoned by a telegraphic message, and started for Shields by the first train that could convey them there; but they were too late. He expired an hour before their arrival.

I need not dwell upon the details of that sad time. Milly felt the blow severely; and it was long before I saw her smile, after that dark December day on which the fatal summons came. She had lost much of her joyousness and brightness after the disappointment about Angus Egerton, and this new sorrow quite crushed her.

They brought Mr. Darrell's remains to Thornleigh, and he was buried in the family vault under the noble old church, where his father and mother, his first wife, and a son who died in infancy had been buried before him. He had been very popular in the neighbourhood, and was sincerely regretted by all who had known him.

Julian Stormont was chief-mourner at the unpretentious funeral. He seemed much affected by his uncle's death; and his manner towards his cousin had an unusual gentleness.

I was present at the reading of the will, which took place in the dining-room immediately after the funeral. Mrs. Darrell, Milly, Mr. Stormont, myself, and the family lawyer were the only persons assembled in the spacious room, which had a dreary look without the chief of the household.

The will had been made a few months after Mr. Darrell's second marriage. It was very simple in its wording. To Julian Stormont he left a sum of five thousand pounds, to be paid out of his funded property; all the rest of this property, with the sum to be realised by the sale of the business at North Shields and its belongings—an amount likely to be very large—was to be divided equally between Mrs. Darrell and her stepdaughter. Thornleigh Manor was left to Mrs. Darrell for her life, but was to revert to Milly, or Milly's heirs, at her death; and Milly was to be entitled to occupy her old home until her marriage.

In the event of Milly's dying unmarried, her share of the funded property was to be divided equally between Mrs. Darrell and Julian Stormont, and in this case the Thornleigh estate was to revert to Julian Stormont after the death of Mrs. Darrell. The executors to the will were Mr. Foreman the lawyer and Mrs. Darrell.

Milly's position was now one of complete independence. Mr. Foreman told her that after the sale of the iron-works she would have an income of something like four thousand a year. She had been of age for more than six months, and there was no one to come between her and perfect independence.

Knowing this, I felt that it was more than probable Mr. Egerton would speedily return to renew his suit; and I had little doubt that it would be successful. I knew how well Milly loved him; and now that her father was gone she could have no motive for refusing him.

'You will stay with me, won't you, Mary?' she said to me as we sat by the fire in mournful silence that afternoon. 'You are my only comfort now, dear. I suppose I shall remain here—for some time, at any rate. Augusta spoke to me very graciously, and begged that I would make this my home, according to my father's wish. We should not interfere with each other in any way, she said, and it was indeed more than probable she would go on the Continent with her maid early in the spring, and leave me sole mistress of Thornleigh. She doubted if she could ever endure the place now, she said. She is not like me, Mary. I shall always have a melancholy love for the house in which I have lived so happily with my father.'

So I remained with my dear girl, and life at Thornleigh Manor glided by in a quiet melancholy fashion. If Mrs. Darrell grieved for her dead husband, her sorrow was of a cold tearless kind; but she kept her own rooms a good deal, and we did not see much of her. The Collingwoods were full of sympathy for their 'darling Milly,' and their affection had some cheering influence upon her mind. From them she heard occasionally of Mr. Egerton, who was travelling in the wildest regions of Northern Europe. She very rarely spoke of him herself at this time; and once when I mentioned his name she checked me reproachfully.

'Don't speak about him, Mary,' she said; 'I don't want to think of him. It seems like a kind of treason against papa. It seems like taking advantage of my dear father's death.'

'Would you refuse to marry him, Milly, if he

were to come back to you, now that you are your own mistress?'

'I don't know that, dear. I think I love him too much to do that. And yet it would seem like a sin against my father.'

The spring months passed, and Milly brightened a little as the days went by. She spent a deal of time amongst the poor; and I think her devotion to that duty helped her to put aside her sorrow more than anything else could have done. I was always with her, sharing in all her work; and I do not believe she had a thought hidden from me at this time.

Mrs. Darrell had not gone abroad yet. She lived a useless, listless life, doing nothing, and caring for nothing, as it seemed. More than once she made preparations for her departure, and then changed her mind at the last moment.

Late in June we heard of Mr. Egerton's return to Cumber; and a few days after that he came to Thornleigh. Mrs. Darrell was in her own room, Milly and I alone in the drawing-room, when he called. My poor girl turned very pale, and the tears came into her eyes as she and Angus Egerton met. He spoke of her loss with extreme delicacy, and was full of tender sympathy. He had news to tell her of himself. A distant relation of his mother's had died lately, leaving him six thousand a year. He had come back to restore Cumber to its old splendour, and to take his proper place in the county.

While they were talking together in low confidential tones, not at all embarrassed by my presence, Mrs. Darrell came into the room. She was paler than usual; but there was an animation in her face that had not been there for a long time. She received Mr. Egerton very graciously, and insisted upon his staying to dinner.

The evening passed very pleasantly. I had never seen Augusta Darrell so agreeable, so fascinating, as she was that night. She touched the piano for the first time since her husband's death, and sang and played with all her old fire, keeping Angus Egerton a prisoner by the side of the piano. Hers was not music to be heard with indifference by the coldest ear.

He came again very soon, and came often. The restorations at Cumber had begun, and he insisted on our driving over to see what he was going to do. We went in compliance with this wish, and I could not but observe how anxiously he questioned Milly as to her opinion of the alterations, and how eagerly he sought for suggestions as to the arrangement and decoration of the different rooms. We spent some hours in this inspection, and stayed to luncheon, in the noble old tapestried drawing-room.

It was not very long before Mr. Egerton had renewed his suit, and had been accepted. Had Mr. Darrell lived, the altered circumstances of the suitor would, in all probability, have made some alteration in his ideas upon this subject. He could no longer have supposed Angus Egerton influenced by mercenary feelings.

My darling seemed perfectly happy in her engagement, and I shared her happiness. I was always to live with her, she said, at Cumber as well as at Thornleigh. She had told Angus this, and he was pleased that it should be so. I thought that she would have no need of me in her wedded days, and that this loving fancy of hers was not likely to be realised; but I allowed her to cherish it—time enough for our parting when it needs must come. My youth had been brightened by her love; and I should be brave enough to face the world alone when she began her new life, assured that in my day of trouble I should always find a haven in her affection.

They were to be married in the following spring.

Mr. Egerton had pleaded hard for an earlier date; but Milly would not diminish her year of mourning for her father, and he was fain to submit. The appointed time was advanced from April to February. He was to take his young wife abroad, and to show her all those scenes in which his wandering life had been spent; and then they were to return to Cumber, and Milly was to begin her career as the wife of a country squire.

Julian Stormont came to Thornleigh, and heard of the engagement from Mrs. Darrell. He still occupied his old position in the business at North Shields, which had been bought by a great capitalist in the iron way. He received the news of Milly's betrothal very quietly; but he proffered her no congratulations upon the subject. I happened to be on the terrace alone with him one morning during his stay, waiting for Milly to join me, when he spoke to me about this business.

'So my cousin is going to throw herself away upon that man?' he said.

'You must not call it throwing herself away, Mr. Stormont,' I answered; 'Mr. Egerton is devoted to your cousin, and the change in his circumstances makes him a very good match for her.'

'The change in his circumstances has not changed the man,' he returned in an angry tone. 'No good can come of such a marriage.'

'You have no right to say that, Mr. Stormont.'

'I have the right given me by conviction. A happy marriage!—no, it will not be a happy marriage, be sure of that!'

He said this with a vindictive look that startled me, well as I knew that he could not feel very kindly towards Milly's lover. The words might mean little, but to me they sounded like a threat.

CHAPTER XI.

DANGER.

THE summer that year was a divine one, and we spent the greater part of our lives out of doors, driving, walking, sitting about the garden sometimes until long after dark. It was weather in which it was a kind of treason against Nature to waste an hour in the house.

We went very often for long rambles in Cumber Wood, winding up with an afternoon tea-drinking in the little study at the Priory—a home-like unceremonious entertainment which Milly delighted in. She used to seem to me on those occasions like some happy child playing at being mistress of the house.

Augusta Darrell was almost always with us. I was sorely puzzled and perplexed by her conduct at this time. It seemed to be all that a kind stepmother's could be. Her old indifferent air had quite vanished; she was more cordial, more affectionately interested in Milly's happiness than I had supposed it possible she could be. The girl was completely melted by the change in her manner, and responded to this new warmth with artless confidence in its reality.

I remembered all I had seen and all I had suspected, and I could not bring myself to believe implicitly in Milly's stepmother. There was a shadowy fear, a vague distrust in my mind, not to be put away.

As I have said, she was always with us, entering into all our simple amusements with an appearance of girlish pleasure. Our picnics, our sketching expeditions, our afternoon tea-parties at the Priory, our croquet-matches with the Rector's daughters, seemed all alike agreeable to her. I noticed that her toilet was always perfect on these occasions, and that she neglected no art which could add to her attractiveness; but she never in any way attempted to absorb Mr. Egerton's attention—she never ignored his position as Milly's accepted suitor.

For a long time I was deceived by her manner—almost convinced that if she had ever cared for Angus Egerton in the past, it was a passion that had died out of her heart. But there came a day when one look of hers betrayed the real state of the case, and showed me that all this newly-awakened regard for

Milly, and pleasant participation in her happiness, had been only a careful piece of acting. It was nothing but a look—one earnest, despairing, passionate look—that told me this, but it was a look that betrayed the secret of a life. From that moment I never again trusted Augusta Darrell.

With the beginning of autumn the weather changed, and there came a dull rainy season. Trouble came to us with the change of the weather. There was a good deal of low fever about Thornleigh, and Milly caught it. She had never neglected her visit amongst the poor, even in favour of those pleasant engagements with Angus Egerton; and there is no doubt she had taken the fever from some of the cottagers.

She was not alarmingly ill, nor was the fever supposed to be contagious, except under certain conditions. Mr. Hale, the Thornleigh doctor, made very light of the business, and assured us that his patient would be as well as ever in a week's time. But in the mean while my dear girl kept her room, and I nursed her, with the assistance of her devoted little maid.

Mr. Egerton came every day, generally twice a day, to inquire about the invalid's progress, and would stay for half an hour, or longer, talking to Mrs.

Darrell or to me. He was very much depressed by this illness, and impatient for his betrothed's recovery. He had been strictly forbidden to see her, as perfect repose was an essential condition to her wellbeing.

The week was nearly over, and Milly had improved considerably. She was now able to sit up for an hour or two every day, and the doctor promised Mr. Egerton that she should be in the drawing-room early in the following week. The weather had been incessantly wet during this time—dull, hopeless, perpetual rain day after day, without a break in the leaden sky. But at last there came a fine evening, and I went down to the terrace to take a solitary walk after my long imprisonment. It was between six and seven o'clock; Milly was asleep, and there was no probability of my being wanted in the sick-room for half an hour or so. I left ample instructions with my handy little assistant, and went down for my constitutional, muffled in a warm shawl.

It was dusk when I went out, and everything was unusually quiet, not a leaf was stirring in the stagnant atmosphere. Late as it was, the evening was almost oppressively warm, and I was glad to throw off my shawl. I walked up and down the terrace in front of the Hall for about ten minutes, and then went round towards the drawing-room windows. Before I had quite reached the first of these, I was arrested by a sound so strange that I stopped involuntarily to listen. Throughout all that followed, I had no time to consider whether I was doing right or wrong in hearing what I did hear; but I believe if I had had ample leisure for deliberation, it would have come to the same thing — I should have listened. What I heard was of such vital consequence to the girl I loved, that I think loyalty to her outweighed any treachery against the speaker.

The strange sound that brought me to a standstill close to the wide-open window was the sound of a woman's passionate sobbing—such a storm of weeping as one does not hear many times in a life. I had never heard anything like it until that night.

Angus Egerton's sonorous voice broke in upon those tempestuous sobs almost angrily:

'Augusta, this is supreme folly.'

The sobs went on for some minutes longer unchecked. I heard his step sounding heavily as he walked up and down the room.

'I am waiting to hear the meaning of all this,' he said by and by. 'I suppose there *is* some meaning.'

'O Angus, is it so easy for you to forget the past?'

'It was forgotten long ago,' he answered, 'by both of us, I should think. When my mother bribed you to leave Ilfracombe, you bartered my love and my happiness for the petty price she was able to pay. I was a weak fool in those days, and I took the business to heart bitterly enough, God knows; but the lesson was a useful one, and it served its turn. I have never trusted myself to love any woman since that day, till I met the pure young creature who is to be my wife. Her truth is above all doubt; she will not sell her birthright for a mess of pottage.'

'The mess of pottage was not for me, Angus. It was my father's bargain, not mine. I was told that you had done with me—that you had never meant to marry me. Yes, Angus, your mother told me that with her own lips—told me that she interfered to save me from misery and dishonour. And then I was hurried off to a cheap French convent, to learn to provide for myself. A couple of years' schooling was the price I received for my broken heart. That was what your mother called making me a lady. I think I should have gone mad in those two dreary years, if it had not been for my passionate love of music. I gave myself up to that with my whole soul; my heart was dead; and they told me I made more progress in two years than other girls made in six. I had nothing else to live for.'

'Except the hope of a rich husband,' said Mr. Egerton, with a sneer.

'O God, how cruel a man can be to a woman he has once loved!' cried Mrs. Darrell passionately. 'Yes, I did marry a rich man, Angus; but I never schemed or tried to win him. The chance came to me without a hope or a thought of mine. It was the chance of rescue from the dreariest life of drudgery that a poor dependent creature ever lived, and I took it. But I have never forgotten you, Angus Egerton, not for one hour of my life.'

'I am sorry you should have taken the trouble to remember me,' he answered very coldly. 'For some years of my life I made it my chief business to forget you, and all the pain connected with our acquaintance; and having succeeded in doing that, it seems a pity that we should disturb the stagnant waters of that dead lake which men call the past.'

'Would to God that we had never met again!' she said.

'I can quite echo that aspiration, if we are likely to have many such scenes as this.'

'Cruel—cruel!' she muttered. 'O Angus, I have been so patient! I have clung to hope in the face of despair. When my husband died I fancied your old love would reawaken. How can such things die? I thought it was to me you would come back—to me, whom you once loved so passionately—not to that girl. You came back to her, and still I was patient. I set myself against her, to win back your love. Yes, Angus, I hoped to do that till very lately. And then I began to see that it was all useless. She is younger and handsomer than I.'

'She is better than you, Augusta. It was not her beauty that won me, but something nobler and rarer than beauty: it was her perfect nature. The more faulty we are ourselves, the more fondly we cling to a good woman. But I don't want to say hard things, Augusta. Pray let us put all this folly aside at once and for ever. You took your course in the past, and it has landed you in a very prosperous position. Let me take mine in the present, and let us be friends, if possible.'

'You know that is not possible. We must be all the world to each other, or the bitterest enemies.'

'I shall never be your enemy, Mrs. Darrell.'

'But I am yours; yes, I am yours from this night, and hers. You think I can look on tamely, and see you devoted to that girl! I have only been playing a part. I thought it was in my power to win you back.'

All this was said with a kind of passionate recklessness, as if the speaker, having suddenly thrown off her mask, scarcely cared how utterly she degraded herself.

'Good-night, Mrs. Darrell. You will think of these things more wisely to-morrow. Let us be civil to each other, at least, while circumstances bring us together; and for God's sake be kind to your stepdaughter! Do not think of her as a rival; my love for you had died long before I saw her. You need bear no malice against her on that account. Goodnight.'

'Good-night.'

I heard the drawing-room door open and shut, and knew that he was gone. I walked on past the open windows, not caring if Mrs. Darrell saw me. It might be better for Milly, perhaps, that she should know I had heard her secret, and had been put upon my guard. But I do not think she saw me.

It was about a quarter of an hour later when I went in, and it was quite dark by that time. In the hall I met Mrs. Darrell, dressed for walking.

'I am going round the shrubberies, Miss Crofton,' she said. 'Insupportably close to-night, is it not? I think we shall all have the fever, if this weather lasts.'

She did not wait for my answer, but passed out quickly. I went back to Milly's room, and found her still sleeping peacefully. Ten minutes afterwards I heard the rain beating against the windows, and knew that it had set in for a wet night.

'Mrs. Darrell will not be able to go far,' I thought.

I sat by the bedside for some time thinking of what I had heard. It was something to have had so strong a proof of Angus Egerton's loyalty to my dear girl; and assured of that, I did not fear Mrs. Darrell's malice. Yet I could not help wishing that the marriage had been appointed for an earlier date, and that the time which stepmother and daughter were to spend together had been shorter.

Milly woke, and sat up for about half an hour, supported by pillows, to take a cup of tea, while I talked to her a little about the pleasantest subjects I could think of. She asked if Mr. Egerton had been at Thornleigh that evening.

'Yes, dear, he has been.'

'Did you see him, Mary?'

'No; I did not see him.'

She gave a little disappointed sigh. It was her delight to hear me repeat his messages to her, word for word, ever so many times over.

'Then you have nothing to tell me about him, dear?'

'Nothing; except that I know he loves you.'

'Ah, Mary, there was a time when you doubted him.'

'That time is quite past and gone, dear.'

She kissed me as she gave me back her cup and saucer, and promised to go to sleep again, while I went to my room to write a long letter home.

I was occupied in this way for more than an hour; and then, having sealed my letter, went down with it to the hall, to put it on a table where all letters intended to be taken to the post in the morning were placed over-night.

It was nearly ten o'clock by this time, and I was startled by the sound of the hall-door opening softly from without, while I was putting down my letter.

I looked round quietly, and saw Mrs. Darrell coming in, with dripping garments.

'Good gracious me!' I cried involuntarily; 'have you been out all this time in the rain, Mrs. Darrell?'

'Yes, I have been out in the rain, Miss Crofton,' she answered in a vexed impatient tone. 'Is that so very shocking to your sober ideas of propriety? I could not endure the house to-night. One has feverish fancies sometimes—at least I have; and I preferred being out in the rain to not being out at all. Good-night.'

She gave me a haughty nod, and ran up-stairs with a quick light step. The old butler came to lock and bolt the hall-door as the clock struck ten, according to unalterable custom; and I went back to my room, wondering what could have kept Mrs. Darrell out so long—whether she had been upon some special errand, or had only been wandering about the grounds in a purposeless way.

For some days Milly went on very well; then there came a little change for the worse. The symptoms were not quite so favourable. Mr. Hale assured us that there was no reason for alarm, the recovery was only a little retarded. He had not the least doubt that all would go well. Mr. Egerton was very quick to take fright, however, and insisted on Dr. Lomond, a famous provincial physician, being summoned immediately from Manchester.

The great man came, and his opinion coincided entirely with that of Mr. Hale. There was not the slightest cause for fear. Careful nursing and quiet were the two essential points. The patient's mind was to be made as happy as possible. The physician made minute inquiries as to the arrangements for attendance in the sick-room, and suggested a professional nurse. But I pleaded so hard against this, assuring him of my capacity for doing much more than I had to do, that he gave way, and consented to Milly being waited on only by myself and her maid.

Mrs. Darrell was present during this conversation, and I was rather surprised by her taking my side of the question with regard to the nursing, as it was her usual habit to oppose me upon all subjects. To-day she was singularly gracious.

Another week went by, and there was no change for the better, nor any very perceptible change for the worse. The patient was a little weaker, and suffered from a depression of mind, against which all my efforts were vain.

Angus Egerton came twice daily during this week, but he rarely saw Mrs. Darrell. I think he studiously avoided meeting her after that painful scene in the drawing-room. It was for me he inquired, and he used to come up-stairs to the corridor outside Milly's room, and stand there talking to me in a low voice, and feeling a kind of satisfaction, I believe, in being so near his darling.

Once I ventured to tell her that he was there, and to let him speak a few words for her to hear. But the sound of the voice she loved so well had such an agitating effect upon her, that I sorely repented my imprudence, and took good care not to repeat it.

So the days went by, in that slow dreary way in which time passes when those we love are ill; and it seemed, in the dead calm of the sick-room, as if all the business of life had come to a stand-still.

I did not see much of Mrs. Darrell during this period. She came to Milly's door two or three times a day to ask about her progress, with all appearance of affection and anxiety; but throughout the rest of the day she remained secluded in her own rooms. I noticed that she had a wan haggard look at this time, like that of a person who had existed for a long while without sleep; but this in no manner surprised me, after that scene in the drawing-room.

As the time went by, I felt that my strength was beginning to fail, and I sadly feared that we might have at last to employ the professional aid which the Manchester physician had suggested. I had slept very little from the beginning of Milly's illness, being too anxious to sleep when I had the opportunity of doing so; and I now began to suffer from the effects of this prolonged sleeplessness. But I struggled resolutely against fatigue, determined to see my dear girl through the fever if possible; and I succeeded wonderfully, by the aid of unlimited cups of strong tea, and always ably seconded by Susan Dodd, Milly's devoted maid.

Between us we two performed all the duties of the sick-room. The medicines, wine, soups, jellies, and all things required for the invalid were kept in the dressing-room, which communicated with the bedroom by one door, and had another door opening on to the corridor.

The sick-room, which was very large and airy, was by this means kept free from all litter; and Susan and I took pleasure in making it look bright and fresh. I used to fetch a bouquet from the garden every morning for the little table by the bed. At the very commencement of Milly's illness I had missed Peter, Mrs. Thatcher's grandson. I asked one of the men what had become of him, and was told that he had taken the fever and was lying ill at his grandmother's cottage. I mentioned this to Mrs. Darrell, and asked her permission to send him some wine and other little comforts, to which she assented.

The Manchester physician came a second time after a week's interval, and on this occasion he was not so positive in his opinion as to the case. He did not consider that there was peril as yet, he said; but the patient was weaker, and he was by no means satisfied. He prescribed a change of medicine, repeated his injunctions about care and quiet; and so departed, after requesting Mr. Hale to telegraph for him in the event of any change for the worse.

I was a good deal depressed by his manner this time, and went back to my dear girl's room with a heavier heart than I had known since her illness began.

It was my habit to take whatever sleep I could in the course of the afternoon, leaving Susan Dodd on guard, so as to be able to sit up all night. Susan had begged very hard to share this night-watching, but I insisted upon her taking her usual rest, so as to be bright and fresh in the day. I felt the night-work was the more important duty, and could trust that to no one but myself.

Unfortunately it happened very often that I was quite unable to sleep when I went to my room in the afternoon to lie down. Half my time I used to lie there wide awake thinking of my darling girl, and praying for her speedy recovery. On the afternoon that followed the Manchester doctor's second visit I went to my room as usual; but I was more than ever disinclined to sleep. For the first time since the fever began I felt a horrible dread that the end might be fatal; and I lay tossing restlessly from side to side, meditating on every word and look of the physician's, and trying to convince myself that there was no real ground for my alarm.

I had been lying awake like this for more than an hour, when I heard the door of Milly's dressing-room—which was close to my door—closed softly; and with a nervous quickness to take alarm I sprang up, and went out into the corridor, thinking that Susan was coming to summon me. I found myself face to face, not with Susan Dodd, but with Mrs. Darrell.

She gave a little start at seeing me, and stood with her hand still upon the handle of the dressing-room door, looking at me with the strangest expression I ever saw in any human countenance. Alarm, defiance, hatred—what was it?

'I thought you were asleep,' she said.

'I have not been able to sleep this afternoon.'

'You are a bad person for a nurse, Miss Crofton, if you cannot sleep at will. I am afraid you are nervous, too, by the way you darted out of the room just now.'

'I heard that door shut, and thought Susan was coming to call me.'

'I had just been in to see how the invalid was going on—that is all.'

She passed me, and went back to her own apartments, which were on the other side of the house. I felt that it was quite useless trying to sleep; so I returned to my room only to change my dressing-gown for my dress, and then went back to Milly. She had been sleeping very quietly, Susan told me.

'I suppose you told Mrs. Darrell that all was going on well when she came to inquire just now?' I said.

'Mrs. Darrell hasn't been since you went to lie down, miss,' the girl answered, looking surprised at my question.

'Why, Susan, you must surely forget. Mrs. Darrell was in the dressing-room scarcely ten minutes ago. I heard her coming out, and went to see who was there. Didn't she come in here to inquire about Miss Darrell?'

'No, indeed, miss.'

'Then I suppose she must have peeped in at the door and seen that Miss Darrell was asleep,' I said.

'I don't see how she could have opened that door without my hearing her, miss. It was shut fast, I know.'

It had been shut when I went in through the dressing-room. I was puzzled by this incident, small as it was. I knew that Augusta Darrell hated her stepdaughter, and I could not bear to think of that secret enemy hovering about the sick-room. I was puzzled too by the look which I had seen in her face —no common look, and not easy to be understood. That she hated me, I had no doubt; but there had been fear as well as aversion in that look, and I could not imagine any possible reason for her fearing such an insignificant person as myself.

The rest of that evening and night passed without any event worth recording. I kept the door of communication between the bedroom and dressing-room wide open all night, determined that Augusta Darrell should not be in that room without my knowledge; but the night passed, and she never came near us.

When I went into the garden early the next morning to gather the flowers for Milly's room, I found Peter at work again. He looked very white and feeble, scarcely fit to be about just yet; but there he was, sweeping the fallen leaves into little heaps, ready for his barrow. He came to me while I was cutting the late roses for my bouquet, and asked after Milly. When I had answered him he loitered by me for a little in a curious way, as if he wanted to say something else; but I was too full of my own thoughts and cares to pay much attention to him.

The next day, and the next, brought no change in my darling, and I was growing every hour more anxious. I could see that Mr. Hale was puzzled and uneasy, though he said he saw no reason for telegraphing to Manchester, yet awhile. He was very attentive, and was reputed to be very clever; and I knew that he was really attached to Milly, whom he had attended from her infancy.

Angus Egerton saw me twice every day; and these brief interviews had now become very painful to me. I found it so difficult to cheer him with hopeful words, when my own heart was hourly growing heavier, and the fears that had been vague and shadowy were gathering strength and shape. I was very tired, but I held out resolutely; and I had never once slept for so much as a quarter of an hour upon my watch, until the second night after that meeting with Mrs. Darrell at the door of the dressing-room.

That night I was seized with an unconquerable sleepiness, about an hour after I had dismissed Susan Dodd. The room was very quiet, not a sound except the ticking of the pretty little clock upon the mantelpiece. Milly was fast asleep, and I was sitting on a low chair by the fire trying to read, when my drowsiness overcame me, my heavy eyelids fell, and I went off into a feverish kind of slumber, in which I was troubled with an uneasy consciousness that I ought to be awake.

I had slept in this way for a little more than an hour, when I suddenly started up broad awake.

the intense quiet of the room I had heard a sound like the chinking of glass, and I fancied that Milly had stirred.

There was a table near her bed, with a glass of cooling drink and a bottle of water upon it. I thought she must have stretched out her hand for this glass, and that in so doing she had pushed the glass against the bottle; but to my surprise I found her lying quite still, and fast asleep. The sound must have come from some other direction—from the dressing-room, perhaps.

I went into the dressing-room. There was no one there. No trace of the smallest disturbance among the things. The medicine-bottles and the medicine-glass stood on the little table exactly as I had left them. I was very careful and precise in my arrangement of these things, and it would have been difficult for the slightest interference with them to have escaped me. What could that sound have been —some accidental shiver of the glass, stirred by a breath of wind, one of those mysterious movements of inanimate objects which are so apt to occur in the dead hours of the night, and which seem always more or less ghostly to a nervous watcher? Could it have been only accidental? or had Mrs. Darrell been prowling stealthily in and out of that room again?

Why should she have been there? What could her secret coming and going mean? What purpose could she have in hovering about the sick girl? what could her hatred profit itself by such uneasy watchfulness, unless— Unless what? An icy coldness came over me, and I shook like a leaf, as a dreadful thought took shape in my mind. What if that desperate woman's hatred took the most awful form? what if her secret presence in that room meant murder?

I took up the medicine-bottle and examined it minutely. In colour, in odour, in taste, the medicine seemed to me exactly what it had been from the time it had been altered, in accordance with the Manchester doctor's second prescription. Mr. Hale's label was on the bottle, and the quantity of the contents was exactly what it had been after I gave Milly her last dose—one dose gone out of the full bottle.

'O, no, no, no,' I thought to myself; 'I must be mad to imagine anything so awful. A woman may be weak, and wicked, and jealous, when she has loved as intensely as this woman seems to have loved

Angus Egerton; but that is no reason she should become a murderess.'

I stood with the medicine-bottle in my hand sorely perplexed. What could I do? Should I suspend the medicine for to-night, at the risk of retarding the cure? or should I give it in spite of that half suspicion that it had been tampered with?

What ground had I for such a suspicion? At that moment nothing but the sound that had awakened me, the chinking sound of one glass knocked against another.

Had I really heard any such sound, or had it only been a delusion of my half sleeping brain? While I stood weighing this question, a sudden recollection flashed across my mind, and I had no longer ground for doubt.

The cork of the medicine-bottle, when I gave Milly her last dose, had been too large for the bottle; so much so, that I had found it difficult to put it in again after giving the medicine. The cork of the bottle which I now held in my hand went in loosely enough. It was a smaller and an older-looking cork. This decided me. I placed the bottle under lock and key in Milly's wardrobe, and I gave her no more medicine that night.

There was no fear of my sleeping at my post after this. My thoughts for the rest of that night were full of horror and bewilderment. My course seemed clear enough, in one respect. The proper person to confide in would be Mr. Hale. He would be able to discover whether the medicine had been tampered with, and it would be his business to protect his patient.

CHAPTER XII.

DEFEATED.

I WENT down to the garden for the flowers as usual next morning, as I did not wish to make any palpable change in my arrangements; but before leaving the room I impressed upon Susan Dodd the necessity of remaining with her mistress during every moment of my absence, though I knew I had little need to counsel carefulness. Nothing was more unlikely than that Susan would neglect her duty for a moment.

Peter came again, as he had come to me on the previous morning. Again he lingered about me, as if he had something more to say, and could not take courage to say it. This time the strangeness of his manner aroused my curiosity, and I asked him if he had anything particular to say to me.

'You must be quick, Peter, whatever it is,' I said; 'for I am in a great hurry to get back to Miss Darrell.'

'There is something I want to say, miss,' he

answered, twisting his ragged straw hat round and round in his bony hands, in a nervous way,—'something I should like to say, but I'm naught but a poor fondy, and don't know how to begin. Only you've been very good to Peter, you see, miss, sending wine and such things when I was ill, and I ain't afeard o' you, as I am o' some folks.'

'The wine was not mine, Peter. Be quick, please; tell me what you want to say.'

'I can't come to it very easy, miss. It's something awful-like to tell on.'

'Something awful?'

The boy had looked round him with a cautious glance, and was now standing close to me, with his light blue eyes fixed upon my face in a very earnest way.

'Speak out, Peter,' I said; 'you needn't be afraid of me.'

'It happened when I was ill, you see, miss, and I've sometimes thought as it might be no more than a dream. I had a many dreams while I were lying on that little bed in grandmother's room, wicked dreams, and this might be one of them; and yet it's real-like, and there isn't the muddle in it that there is in the other dreams.'

'What is it, Peter? O, pray, pray be quick!'

'I'm a-coming to it, miss. Is it wicked for folks to kill theirselves?'

'Is it wicked? Of course it is — desperately wicked; a sin that can never be repented of.'

'Then I know one that's going to do it.'

'Who?'

'Mrs. Darrell.'

He gave a solemn nod, and stood staring at me with wide-open awe-stricken eyes.

'How do you know that?'

'It was one dark night, when it was raining hard—I could hear it drip, drip, drip upon the roof just over where I was lying. It was when I was very bad, and lay still all day and couldn't speak. But I knew what grandmother said to me, and I knew everything that was going on, though I didn't seem to — that was the curious part of it. I had been asleep for a bit, and I woke up all of a sudden, and heard some one talking to grandmother in the next room — the door wasn't wide open, only ajar. I shouldn't have known who it was, for I'm not quick at telling voices, like other folks; but I heard grandmother call her Mrs. Darrell; and I heard the lady say that when one was sick and tired of life, and had no one left to live for, it was best to die; and grandmother laughed, and says yes, there wasn't much to live for, leastways not for such as her. And then they talked a little more; and then by and by Mrs. Darrell asked her for some stuff—I didn't hear the name of it, for Mrs. Darrell only whispered it. Grandmother says no, and stuck to it for a good time; but Mrs. Darrell offered her money, and then more and more money. She says it couldn't matter whether she got the stuff from her or from any one else. She could get it easily enough, she says, in any large town. And she didn't know as she should use it, she says. It was more likely than not she never would; but she wanted to have it by her, so as to feel she was able to put an end to her life, if ever it grew burdensome to her. "You'll never use it against any one else?" says grandmother; and Mrs. Darrell says who was there she could use it against, and what harm need she wish to anybody; she was rich enough, and had nothing to gain from anybody's death. So at last, after a deal of talk, grandmother gave her the stuff; and I heard her counting out money—I think it was a hundred pounds—and then she went away in the rain.'

I remembered that night upon which Mrs. Dar

rell had stayed out so long in the rain—the night that followed her stormy interview with Angus Egerton.

I told Peter that he had done quite right in telling me this, and begged him not to mention it to any one else until I gave him permission to do so. I went back to Milly's room directly afterwards, and waited there for Mr. Hale's coming.

While I was taking my breakfast, Mrs. Darrell came to make her usual inquiries. I ran into the dressing-room to meet her. While she was questioning me about the invalid, I saw her look at the table where the medicine had always been until that morning, and I knew that she missed the bottle.

After she had made her inquiries, she stood for a few moments hesitating, and then said abruptly,

'I should like to see Mr. Hale when he comes this morning. I want to hear what he says about his patient. He will be here almost immediately, I suppose; so I will stay in Milly's room till he comes.'

She went into the bedroom, bent over the invalid for a few minutes, talking in a gentle sympathetic voice, and then took her place by the bedside. It was evident to me that she had suspected something from the removal of the medicine, and that she intended to prevent my seeing Mr. Hale alone.

'You took your medicine regularly last night, I suppose, Milly?' she inquired presently, when I had seated myself at a little table by the window and was sipping my tea.

'I don't think you gave me quite so many doses last night, did you, Mary?' said the invalid, in her feeble voice. 'I fancy you were more merciful than usual.'

'It was very wrong of Miss Crofton to neglect your medicine. Mr. Hale will be extremely angry when he hears of it.'

'I do not think Milly will be much worse for the omission,' I answered quietly.

After this we sat silently waiting for the doctor's appearance. He came in about a quarter of an hour, and pronounced himself better pleased with his patient than he had been the night before. There had been a modification of the more troublesome symptoms of the fever towards morning.

I told him of my omission to give the medicine.

'That was very wrong,' he said.

'Yet you see she had a better night, Mr. Hale. I suppose that medicine was intended to modify those attacks of sickness from which she has suffered so much ?'

'To prevent them altogether, if possible.'

'That is very strange. It really appears to me that the medicine always increases the tendency to sickness.'

Mr. Hale shook his head impatiently.

'You don't know what you are talking about, Miss Crofton,' he said.

'May I say a few words to you alone, if you please ?'

Mrs. Darrell rose, with a hurried anxious look.

'What can you have to say to Mr. Hale alone, Miss Crofton ?' she asked.

'It is about herself, perhaps,' said the doctor kindly. 'I have told her all along that she would be knocked up by this nursing; and now I daresay she begins to find I am right.'

'Yes,' I said, 'it is about myself I want to speak.'

Mrs. Darrell went to one of the windows, and stood with her face turned away from us, looking out. I followed Mr. Hale into the dressing-room.

I unlocked the wardrobe, took out the medicine-bottle, and told the doctor my suspicions of the previous night. He listened to me with grave attention, but with an utterly incredulous look.

'A nervous fancy of yours, no doubt, Miss Crofton,' he said; 'however, I'll take the medicine back to my surgery and analyse it.'

'I have something more to tell you, Mr. Hale.'

'Indeed!'

I repeated, word for word, what Peter had told me about Mrs. Darrell's visit to his grandmother.

'It is a very extraordinary business,' he said; 'but I cannot imagine that Mrs. Darrell would be capable of such a hideous crime. What motive could she have for such an act?'

'I do not feel justified in speaking quite plainly upon that subject, Mr. Hale; but I have reason to know that Mrs. Darrell has a very bitter feeling about her stepdaughter.'

'I cannot think the thing you suspect possible. However, the medicine shall be analysed; and we will take all precautions for the future. I will send you another bottle immediately, in a sealed packet. You will take notice that the seal is unbroken before you use the medicine.'

He showed me his crest on a seal at the end of his pencil-case, and then departed. The medicine came a quarter of an hour later in a sealed packet. This time I brought the bottle into the sick-room, and placed it on the mantelpiece, where it was impossible for any one to touch it.

When Mr. Hale came for his second visit, there was a grave and anxious look in his face. He was very well satisfied with the appearance of the patient, however, and pronounced that there was a change for the better—slight, of course, but quite as much as could be expected in so short a time. He beckoned me out of the room, and I went down-stairs with him, leaving Susan Dodd with Milly.

'I am going to speak to Mrs. Darrell, and you had better come with me,' he said.

She was in the library. Mr. Hale went in, and I followed him. She was sitting at the table, with writing materials scattered before her; but she was not writing. She had a strange preoccupied air; but at the sight of Mr. Hale she rose suddenly, and looked at him with a deadly white face.

'Is she worse?' she asked.

'No, Mrs. Darrell; she is better,' he answered sternly. 'I find that we have been the dupes of some secret enemy of this dear child's. There has been an attempt at murder going on under our very eyes. Poison has been mixed with the medicine sent by me—a slow poison. Happily for us the poisoner has been a little too cautious for the success of the crime. The doses administered have been small enough to leave the chance of recovery. An accident awakened Miss Crofton's suspicions last night, and she very wisely discontinued the medicine. I have analysed it since she gave it me, and find that a certain portion of irritant poison has been mixed with it.'

For some moments after he had finished speaking Mrs. Darrell remained silent, looking at him fixedly with that awful death-like face.

'Who can have done such a thing?' she asked at last, in a half-mechanical way.

'You must be a better judge of that question than I,' answered Mr. Hale. 'Is there any one in this house inimical to your stepdaughter?'

'No one, that I know of.'

'We have two duties before us, Mrs. Darrell: the first, to protect our patient from the possibility of any farther attempt of this kind; the second, to trace the hand that has done this work. I shall telegraph to Leeds immediately for a professional nurse, to relieve Miss Crofton in the care of the sick-room;

and I shall communicate at once with the police, in order that this house may be placed under surveillance.'

Mrs. Darrell said not a word, either in objection or assent, to this. She seated herself by the table again, and began trifling idly with the writing materials before her.

'You will do what is best, of course, Mr. Hale,' she said, after a long pause; 'you are quite at liberty to act in this matter according to your own discretion.'

'Thanks; it is a matter in which my responsibility entitles me to a certain amount of power. I shall telegraph to Dr. Lomond, asking him to come down to-morrow. Whatever doubt you may entertain of my judgment will be dispelled when I am supported by his opinion.'

'Of course; but I have not expressed any doubt of your judgment.'

We left her immediately after this—left her sitting before the table, with her restless hands turning over the papers.

The servant who went in search of her at seven o'clock that evening, when dinner was served, found her sitting there still, with a sealed letter lying on the table before her; but her head had fallen across the cushioned arm of the chair—she had been dead some hours.

There was a post-mortem examination and an inquest. Mrs. Darrell had taken poison. The jury brought in a verdict of suicide while in a state of unsound mind. The act seemed too causeless for sanity. Her strange absent ways had attracted the attention of the servants for some time past, and the evidence of her own maid respecting her restlessness and irritability for the last few months influenced the minds of coroner and jury.

The letter found lying on the table before her was addressed to Angus Egerton. He declined to communicate its contents when questioned about it at the inquest. Milly progressed towards recovery slowly but surely from the hour in which I stopped the suspected medicine. The time came when we were obliged to tell her of her stepmother's awful death; but she never knew the attempt that had been made on her own life, or the atmosphere of hatred in which she had lived.

We left Thornleigh for Scarborough as soon as she was well enough to be moved, and only returned in the early spring, in time for my darling's wedding.

She has now been married nearly seven years, during which time her life has been very bright and happy—a life of almost uncheckered sunshine. She has carried out her idea of our friendship to the very letter; and we have never been separated, except during her honeymoon and my own visits home. Happily for my sense of independence, there are now plenty of duties for me to perform at Cumber Priory, where I am governess to a brood of pretty children, who call me auntie, and hold me scarcely second to their mother in their warm young hearts. Angus Egerton is a model country squire and master of the hounds; and he and his wife enjoy an unbroken popularity among rich and poor. Peter is under-gardener at the Priory, and no longer lives with his grandmother, who left her cottage soon after Mrs. Darrell's suicide, and is supposed to have gone to London.

OLD RUDDERFORD HALL

CHAPTER I.

OLD RUDDERFORD HALL lay back from the high-road, buried in trees, and all the traveller saw of it was a glimpse of mellow red-brick chimney, or an angle of the steep tiled roof, above oaks and elms that had been growing ever since the Norman Conquest, when all about the trim little out-of-the-world village of Rudderford was forest land.

New Rudderford Hall fronted the turnpike road, resplendent with three rows of shining plate-glass windows, a brilliant stuccoed front, a conservatory with a glass dome flashing in the summer sun, a prim lawn embellished with geometrical flower-beds, all ablaze with scarlet and yellow, and two pair of bran-new Birmingham iron gates, of florid design, surmounted by two pair of lamps. New Rudderford Hall looked what it was—the abode of commercial wealth. New Rudderford Hall gave dinner-parties, a ball once a year, hunting-breakfasts in the late autumn, private theatricals at Christmas. New Rudderford Hall had three rosy daughters and one stalwart hard-riding son, the apple of its eye.

Old Rudderford Hall rarely opened its rusty gates or unlocked its creaking doors. There was, indeed, a legend that no stranger had broken bread there for a century; yet there was a counter-story current to the effect that the master of Old Rudderford Hall could, when he chose, open a bottle of rare old wine for a visitor—Madeira that had voyaged three times to and fro the East Indies; golden-tinted Tokay; red and white Constantia; Malmsey that seemed so old it might have formed part of the contents of that ancient hogshead wherein poor Clarence elected to be drowned. Old Rudderford Hall had one only child, a daughter, fair to see, who rode an ancient purblind palfrey about the shady lanes round Rudderford, and was met sometimes in the dwellings of the poor, but never in that exalted sphere which Rudderford called 'society.' Old Rudderford Hall rejoiced in that patrician appendage — a family ghost.

The story went that a Champion of the days of the Stuarts had slain his wife in some fit of jealous fury, and that the poor lady's restless spirit—the legend hinted at her guilt—haunted the long dark passages and dismal chambers of the old house. It was not very clear that any one had ever seen her, but she was firmly believed in nevertheless, and plenty of people were able to give a graphic description of her—a tall graceful lady, dressed in white, with flowing auburn hair falling over her neck and shoulders.

The present owner of the Hall was Anthony Champion, and the estate had belonged to the house of Champion ever since the days of Henry VIII., who, in the distribution of church property, had rewarded his liege servant, Thomas Champion, gentleman, for divers services not set down in the title-deeds of the estate, with the copyhold of Rudderford Chase and Rudderford Grange, previously held by a monkish fraternity settled in the neighbourhood.

There were portions of the old Grange still standing—massive stone walls pierced with narrow arched windows, a winding staircase, and low oak door, iron-bound and studded with huge nails; but these stone buildings now served only as offices, and the Hall proper had been built by the aforesaid Thomas Champion, with much splendour and lavish expenditure, in an age when architectural extravagance had been made fashionable by the magnificent Wolsey.

The house was one of the finest specimens of domestic architecture in England, but had been sorely neglected for the last century. Wherever decay could arise, it had arisen, and a settled gloom had fallen upon the mansion and its surroundings. Only in the flower-garden was there any glimpse of neatness or brightness, and that was due to the care of Christabel Champion, who loved the old flower-beds, the grassy walks, and ancient roses, and who not only superintended the labours of a great hulking lad of seventeen, sole gardener at the Hall, but worked hard herself into the bargain.

Within, the gloom was almost oppressive. Anthony Champion was a man who lived amongst his books, and dreamed away his days over mouldy old folios and rare editions collected by his father, when the Champion purse was deeper than it was nowadays. He lived almost wholly in his library, only emerging at seven in the evening to share his daughter's frugal dinner, and to doze or muse for an hour or so afterwards in the long saloon. There was some little show of state and ceremony kept up at the Hall, though there were only three servants in a house where there had once been forty—an ancient butler and housekeeper, man and wife, and a buxom country girl, who did all the scrubbing and cleaning, attended to a small dairy, and waited upon Christabel.

The master of Old Rudderford Hall was as poor as Job in his day of affliction; or at least so ran the common rumour, amply sustained by the mode and manner of his existence. A hundred years ago there had been revelry and splendour at the grand old house, but at that time a great misfortune befell its master, in the untimely death of his eldest son, killed in a duel; and the bereaved father shut up the house, and went to France, where he lived a wild life, and squandered a noble fortune at the profligate court of Louis the Well-beloved. He died in Paris a year or so before the revolution, which was to regenerate mankind, arrived at that stage in which it began to improve them off the face of the earth; and probably by his timely decease escaped a ruder exit *viâ* the guillotine. His estate, much impoverished, descended to a nephew, a studious young man, lame and of feeble health, who married a girl of humble birth, lived the life of a recluse in the neglected house, and became the father of Anthony Champion, the present master of the old Hall.

It is possible that, when young Anthony inherited the estate, shrunk and burdened as it was, he might have made some effort to brighten and improve things, if fortune had favoured him ever so little. But again did affliction fall heavily upon the old house. He married a woman he adored, a fair young girl of high family but no fortune, and brought her home to the Hall, full of all manner of schemes for the future. For a little more than a year he lived a life of supreme domestic happiness, and then— two months after the birth of a baby-girl—he saw an unusual flush upon his young wife's cheek one day, and the next beheld her stricken with typhus-fever. In a week all was over, and he stood alone by his dreary hearth, like a strong man turned to stone. It was long before the caresses of his child could bring the faintest shadow of a smile to his haggard face. He seemed to grow an old man all at once. Unlike his ancestor, he did not turn his back upon the scene of his suffering; he only entombed himself there, buried alive among his books. He had inherited his father's studious habits; and after a weary year, in which he sat alone day after day, helpless, hopeless, blankly staring at the wall before him, and brooding over his misery, he grew to find some cold comfort in recondite studies of so close and severe a kind, that the more credulous among his neighbours talked of him darkly as of something not quite canny.

For such a man society could have no charm. Had he possessed the wealth of all the Rothschilds, he would have lived very much as he did live. A retinue of servants might have eaten and drunk at his expense, a vast amount of splendid upholstery might have been created at his cost; but his individual expenditure would have been no greater, his manner of existence no more cheerful. He lived alone by choice; and so utterly narrowed had his mind become by constant brooding on one vain regret, as to make him half-unconscious that this hermit life was scarcely the best and brightest for a girl of eighteen. The motherless baby whose plaintive cries had rent his heart years ago had blossomed into a lovely girl, painfully like his lost wife. Long and dreary as his days and nights had seemed to him ever since *that* loss, he had been scarcely conscious of the actual progress of time. The lapse might be five years or fifty. It was a surprise to him to see his daughter grown to womanhood. He woke up from a long sleep, as it were, and looked at her with vague wonder. Seven or eight years before, he had made a friendly arrangement with the rector's wife, by which Christabel was to share the studies of the four girls at the rectory, under an admirable governess; and by virtue of this arrangement his daughter's education had cost him very little money and no trouble.

He loved her fondly, and yet had given her little of his confidence. Rarely did he see the fair young face looking up at him without a faint pang, which was like the memory of an acute agony rather than actual present pain. She was so like her mother! He fancied sometimes how fair a picture those two faces would have made side by side—one developed and matronly, the other in all the bloom of girlhood.

She had her little circle of friends—a very small one. The only house she visited was the rectory, and there she came and went like a daughter of the house. There she had met the New Rudderford Hall people—Frank Greenwood and his three sisters, who fell in love with her—the sisters, that is to say—at first sight. Frank said very little about her. She declined all invitations to their parties, however—indeed, she had none of the finery required for such occasions—but consented to join them now and then on the croquet-lawn and share their afternoon tea.

CHAPTER II.

New Rudderford Hall was built upon a part of the land which King Henry bestowed upon his liege Thomas Champion, and this fact was resented by Anthony as a personal offence against him upon the part of Mr. Greenwood. If he had been a visiting man even, nothing could have induced him to break bread with the master of the new Hall, and he always heard of his daughter's intimacy with 'those Greenwood girls' with displeasure.

'I can't imagine what induces you to cultivate such people, Christabel,' he said fretfully, as they were sitting together in the summer dusk after dinner one evening in the long saloon—a melancholy room which would have comfortably accommodated an assembly of fifty, and seemed very dreary in its faded splendour, occupied only by the father and daughter.

'I never have cultivated them, papa. You know

how many invitations they have sent me, and I have declined them all.'

'You have been to their house.'

'Yes, to play croquet, now and then; never to any of their parties.'

'I suppose that is a deprivation,' said Mr. Champion, with a sigh. 'I daresay there are people who would call me a cruel father, and the life you lead in this old house an unnatural one.'

'Pray, pray, don't say that, my dear father,' cried the girl earnestly, coming over to his chair by the open window, and laying her hand carelessly upon his shoulder. You know that I am quite content to be with you; there is no higher happiness I could desire than that. If our lives are a little dull sometimes, and one is subject to an occasional attack of low spirits, never mind; there are other times when life seems all sunshine, and the garden and the dear old house enchanted, like the fairy palace in *Beauty and the Beast*. Why, after all, my life is quite as gay as Beauty's was. As long as you like to live alone, papa, I will be content with our solitude; though I confess it would make me happy to see you go more into the world.'

The world, in Christabel's ideas, meant Rudderford, and half-a-dozen houses within half-a-dozen miles of Rudderford. Perhaps the world of which she was thinking just at this moment meant even something less than that—an occasional dinner-party at Samuel Greenwood's smart stuccoed mansion.

'That is a sight you will never see, my dear,' answered her father drearily. 'I shut my door upon the world when I came home from your mother's funeral—home! and she was no longer there! No, Christabel; the world and I have parted company too long for any sympathy to be possible between us. A man coming out into the clamour and confusion of Paris after five-and-twenty years in one of the underground cells of the Bastille could not feel himself more a stranger than I should, if I were to go into the world now. But I am not going to keep you buried alive for ever. You have blossomed into a woman all at once, and taken me by surprise. I want a little time to think about it, and then I shall form some plan for giving you a brighter life.'

'I don't wish for any change, papa. I would not leave you for the world. If you have any plan for sending me away, pray abandon it. Not all the pleasures in the world would make up to me for leaving you. Indeed, indeed, I am quite happy!

I have my poor people to visit, and—and—a few friends'—she hesitated, with a sudden blush, remembering that those obnoxious Greenwoods were among the few—' and my dear old horse, Gilpin.'

Mr. Champion smiled at the mention of this last item.

'Gilpin is scarcely a steed for a young lady to boast of,' said he. 'I suppose the world thinks that I can give you no better mount than old Gilpin; that I live the life I do from poverty as much as for any other reason.'

'People may think so, papa; what does it matter?'

'Nothing, child; but for once the world is out in its reckoning. I am not a poor man. The estate was heavily burdened when I succeeded to it, but money has accumulated rapidly in the life I have led, and I have paid off everything—have saved money, too. If I could have only bought back the land upon which the new Hall stands, and pulled down that vulgar cockney house, I should think my money worth something; but that's out of the question. Samuel Greenwood is one of the richest men in the county, and would dearly like to buy me out of this place. However, don't let's talk of him; the subject always puts me out of temper. When the time comes for your marrying, Christabel, you will not be a penniless bride.'

'I hope, if ever I do marry, papa, it will be some one who won't care whether I have any money or not.'

'Of course; that's a girl's notion. But people do care. I don't want you to marry a pauper who, having nothing to bestow, would be content to take you with nothing. The age has grown commercial, my dear; the more money a man has, the more he expects with his wife. And when you go into society by and by, as I intend you shall do, you shall appear as becomes a gentleman's daughter; and when you marry, you shall have such jewels as not one woman in a hundred can show.'

'Jewels, papa!' cried Christabel, opening her blue eyes to their widest extent—'jewels!'

Except a white cornelian necklace and a gold heart-shaped locket containing her mother's hair, the girl had never possessed a trinket in her life.

'Yes, child, jewels. Stay here a minute, and I'll show you something.'

There was a door at one end of the saloon opening into the library, that darksome den in which

Anthony Champion spent his days, and which was rarely invaded by the foot of the industrious housemaid. A dingy old room, lined from floor to ceiling with dingy books—books in piles on the floor, books on the mantelpiece, books heaped up on the three broad oak window-seats, books everywhere, and between the windows two huge carved-oak muniment chests.

Anthony left his daughter in the saloon, and went into the library. He unlocked one of these muniment chests, and took out a battered old leather-covered box, which had once been crimson. This he brought to Christabel. There was just light enough for her to see some faded gilt lettering at top, the initials 'C. C.'

'Was that my mother's?' she asked, scrutinising those two letters with interest.

'No. This jewel-case belonged to my great-aunt Caroline Champion, the mother of that unhappy lad who lost his life in a drunken brawl which ended in bloodshed. When Angus Champion turned his back upon Rudderford, he left this box behind him—forgot its existence, perhaps; who knows? His wife had been dead nine years. At any rate, although he spent almost everything he could lay his hands upon, the jewels remained in an iron safe in the steward's room, among old leases and useless parchments, and there my father found them when he inherited the property. As they had escaped so long, he did not care to sell them. "My son's wife shall wear them," he said. But your mother never lived to wear them, Christabel. We used to talk merrily enough of the day when she should be presented at court, in a blaze of diamonds. Yet she wore no ornaments but the roses we put in her coffin.' He stopped for a few moments: *that* memory never came to him without the familiar pang. 'And now I am going to dazzle your eyes,' he said, putting aside the bitter thought with an effort. There are loves that do verily last a lifetime, and his was one of those.

He unlocked the jewel-case, and lifted the lid. Christabel gave a great cry of rapture. There was a tray of diamonds—necklace, bracelets, brooch, earrings, set in silver, in a solid simple style. The stones were large and brilliant, perfect in colour, of a greater value than Anthony Champion imagined, though he deemed them worth a round sum.

He raised the upper tray, and revealed a lower one, full of sapphires in a quaint filigree gold setting; then he showed his daughter another tray, containing a necklace and earrings of amethysts and pearls, which Christabel declared were more beautiful than the diamonds; and then the bottom of the box, in which there were only odds and ends—antique rings, an apostle's spoon, a smelling-bottle, a couple of thimbles, a fruit-knife, a locket, a brooch or two, and so on. But these interested Christabel almost more than the precious stones, and she sat looking them over entranced, with the three jewel-trays spread out upon the table.

'Hark!' said her father suddenly. 'What was that?'

'What, papa?'

'That noise outside; it sounded like a step upon the gravel. Look out, Christabel, and see if there is any one.'

Miss Champion stepped out of the long window. There was a wide gravel walk before the saloon windows, somewhat weedy and moss-grown, and beyond that a shrubbery where the young firs and shrubs grew thick and tall—a shrubbery in which a dozen men might have hidden securely enough.

There was no one to be seen. The girl glanced up and down the weedy walk, very desolate-looking in the summer twilight, and peered into the shrubbery, parting the thick laurels here and there, but without result.

'Are you sure you heard a footstep, papa?' she asked rather incredulously, as she came back to the room.

'Yes,' said Mr. Champion, who had been hastily replacing the jewel-trays while his daughter was looking about, 'I am sure. And there was something more than a footstep. I saw a shadow fall across the window.'

'The shadow of a tree, perhaps, papa.'

'There is no tree that can cast a shadow on this window. It was gone in a moment. There has been some one watching us, Christabel.'

'A tramp, perhaps, papa,' said Miss Champion coolly.

The approaches to Old Rudderford Hall were ill guarded—guarded not at all, in fact. The gates were never locked, and for those intruders who might find the legitimate mode of entrance inconvenient, there were numerous gaps in the fence through which they might roam into the park at will.

Plenty of tramps therefore came to the old Hall, and were wont to depart protesting against the inhospitality of the back door and kitchen department in general. There were no beer-drinking grooms to wheedle out of a friendly pint; no gossiping scullery-maids to give them bread and cheese or broken victuals—the bone of a leg of mutton and half a loaf of bread, or the carcasses of a pair of fowls and a dish of cold vegetables. There was nothing to be heard or seen, no hen-roosts to be robbed—for the poultry-yard was a desert: only closely-shut doors, and blank iron-barred windows; weeds growing between the flagstones in the court, an empty dog-kennel, a locked dairy, a broken pump, which would not yield the wanderer so much as the refreshment of a draught of spring water.

'A tramp!' exclaimed Mr. Champion with displeasure. 'I'm afraid you encourage such vermin by your indiscriminate charities, Christabel.'

Christabel looked downward with a faint little sigh. If not a miser in theory, Mr. Champion had been a miser in practice; and so restricted was her pocket-money, that these indiscriminate charities of which he complained consisted of a stray sixpence now and then bestowed upon some footsore vagrant, whose piteous tale touched the tender young heart.

'A tramp!' repeated Mr. Champion: 'a pleasant thing for a tramp to have seen those jewels. I'll put them away this moment, and do you look out again, Christabel, and see if you can discover any one lurking about; and you might tell David to keep his eyes open.'

David was the solitary gardener and out-of-door man, who had the custody of grounds that could have been barely kept in order by six.

Miss Champion stepped out into the garden again under a darkening sky, and this time looked more closely than before, making a circuit of the shrubbery by a path half choked with the wild growth of neglected shrubs, going round into the old Dutch garden, glancing even into the kitchen garden beyond, where she found David staring pensively into a broken cucumber frame.

To him she gave her father's order, which he received almost contemptuously.

'Tramps, miss! Lor' a mercy, they don't do no harm. There's nothing for 'em to steal.'

Of course the intruder, whoever he might be must have had ample time to make his escape after Mr. Champion first took alarm. David prowled slowly through the gardens, stared across a massive holly hedge into the park, saw no one, and wended his solitary way to the house to report accordingly.

CHAPTER III.

CHRISTABEL met Rosa Greenwood next morning in one of the green lanes beyond the village when she was returning from a long ramble on Gilpin, and that young lady told her of a croquet party that was to take place at New Rudderford Hall that evening, and to which she must certainly come.

'It's not the least bit in the world a party, you know, dear,' Miss Greenwood pleaded, patting Gilpin's iron-gray shoulder; ' quite an impromptu affair got up for Miss Perkington, only daughter of the great firm of Perkington and Tanberry, cloth manufacturers, who is staying with us. *Such* a dear girl; not exactly pretty, but *so* interesting. We all want Frank to marry her, and I really think she likes him. But there's no knowing; young men are so peculiar.'

Christabel wore a straw hat with a blue veil, and under the blue veil the roses on her cheeks deepened a little at this juncture.

'Now you must, must, must come, Christabel. I won't accept a refusal. The rectory girls are to be with us. We are to dine at five, so as to secure a long evening, and begin croquet at six; and we can wind up with a waltz or two before supper.'

Christabel's eyes quite sparkled at the idea of a waltz. Dancing was a dissipation which seemed to her inexperience the height of earthly felicity. She had waltzed all by herself on the lawn many a summer evening, softly singing some languorous melody of D'Albert's as she danced.

'I should dearly like to come,' she said thoughtfully, 'but I don't know if papa—'

'Papa! bosh!' exclaimed Miss Greenwood, who was somewhat fast and irreverent in her notions of parental authority. 'I should like to see the author of *my* being putting a spoke in the wheel if I wanted to enjoy myself. As if your life wasn't dull enough, mewed up in that dreary old Hall!' And Miss Greenwood made a wry face, which expressed her supreme contempt for the grand old Tudor mansion, as compared with the smart plate-glass-windowed habitation which sheltered her fair self.

'I'll ask papa if I may come at eight,' said Christabel. 'He dines at seven, you know, and he always likes to have me with him at dinner. I couldn't possibly come *till* eight; but the evenings are so long now.'

'It's a great deal too late,' replied Rosa, flicking a fly off Gilpin's nose. 'However, if you must stop to see that curious old pa of yours eat his dinner, you must. But remember we shall expect you at eight sharp. I'll send Frank to meet you at the field-gate.'

'O, please don't,' cried Christabel.

'But I please shall. He'll meet you at the gate when the clock strikes eight.'

Miss Champion walked her horse to the end of the lane, Rosa Greenwood walking by her side, telling her about that wonderful young person Miss Victoria Perkington, who, by virtue of her position as the only daughter of Perkington and Tanberry, had an allowance which made the condition of the rich Miss Greenwoods seem absolute penury.

'You should see the dresses she has brought with her for a ten days' visit!' exclaimed Rosa. 'A basket as big as a house, and all of them from a Frenchwoman in Bruton-street. There's a corded black silk trimmed with white lace—Valenciennes—three inches deep on all the flounces and puffings; worth a fortune—a perfect duck of a dress!'

Christabel thought of her jewels, and wished that

she could have melted just a few of those diamonds, which she could never wear till she was married, into silk dresses. She gave a little sigh, thinking of the scantiness of her wardrobe, and how very poor a figure she must needs seem in the eyes of Miss Perkington, and rode slowly home, meditative, and not altogether happy.

'I daresay he will marry her,' she said to herself. 'It is just as papa said last night. The richer people are, the more eager they are to increase their wealth. He will marry her no doubt, and buy some great estate in the neighbourhood, and build a big ugly house; and I shall see them riding by on their thorough-bred horses, and laughing at poor old Gilpin.'

She bent over her horse's neck to pat him at this thought, and one childish tear dropped upon the iron-gray mane. She was not much more than a child, and Frank Greenwood had been very tender and deferential in his manner to her always. It gave her a sharp pain to think that he would pass quite out of her life, and belong to Miss Perkington.

'Would you object to my going to play croquet at—at the new Hall this evening, papa?' the girl asked timidly, during dinner.

'Object? Well, my dear, you know I detest those

Greenwood people'—it is doubtful if he had seen them three times in his life—'but I suppose it would be hard upon you to forbid your enjoying any little pleasure they may offer you in a quiet way. It is not a party, of course?'

'O no, papa. I only heard of it from Rosa when I was out this morning.'

'Mind, I set my face absolutely against your appearance at any of their ostentatious parties. I'll not have *my* daughter paraded at Samuel Greenwood's chariot-wheels. But as far as a game of croquet goes, if it pleases you, I've no objection.'

'Thanks, dear papa.'

'When are you going?'

'Directly after dinner.'

'That will be eight o'clock. I shall send David for you at half-past nine.'

Only an hour and a half! Would there be time for those waltzes on the lawn? She had danced several times with Frank at that hospitable rectory, and knew that he was an agreeable partner.

'There is to be a kind of supper, I believe, papa,' she faltered.

'A kind of supper? Say ten, then, or half-past at the latest.'

'Thank you, dear papa.'

'Bless my heart! one would think these people were the most congenial acquaintance you could desire.'

'The rectory girls are to be there, papa,' Christabel said demurely.

'Well, I don't wonder at your being attached to *them*. Run away, child, and dress yourself. I can finish my dinner alone.'

Miss Champion kissed her father, and tripped away to make her brief toilet; pleased, and yet with a vague pain at her heart—a pain that was associated with the image of the unknown Miss Perkington. Rosa Greenwood had called her brother 'peculiar' in a tone that seemed to imply his indifference to the great heiress; but she had not said the marriage was at all unlikely: and the family wished it; and Miss Perkington was *there;* and Frank was a man of the world—very bright and clever, and open-hearted, but a man of the world nevertheless.

She put on her white-muslin dress—a dress three summers old, which had been lengthened artfully, but not imperceptibly, to suit her increasing height; just such a dress as must of necessity provoke contempt in the mind of Miss Perkington, who of course had never in her life worn anything lengthened or 'let out.' She tied a broad blue ribbon round her slim white throat, with the gold heart-shaped locket hanging to it, and then looked at herself in the glass discontentedly. It was a very beautiful picture which she saw in that old-fashioned cheval glass—a tall, slender, white-robed figure, and a fair young face framed in luxuriant auburn hair; but Christabel only saw the deficiencies of her costume, and turned away from the glass with a sigh.

Her father was dozing in his deep armchair when she peeped into the saloon to bid him good-bye; so she went lightly out of the window and away through the gardens, into a meadow where a solitary cow was browsing in the still evening atmosphere, and on to that field-gate of which Miss Greenwood had spoken; a gate that divided Samuel Greenwood's territory from the shrunken lands of the Champions.

Rudderford Church clock chimed the three-quarters after seven as Christabel crossed the meadow. She was just a quarter of an hour before the time appointed. She was half glad, half sorry, to think that Frank would not be there.

He was there, nevertheless—a good-looking young fellow, sitting on the gate in a contemplative attitude, thinking so profoundly, that he looked up with a start as the light footstep came close to him—a start, and something like a blush.

'How good of you to come so early!' he said, as they shook hands, and he held the little hand an extra moment or so. (It was just the sort of meeting in which a young man would consider himself entitled to one gentle pressure before he released a pretty girl's hand.) 'I strolled over here ten minutes ago to have a good think. I don't often think; it's a bad habit.'

Christabel laughed. She was almost always gay in his presence; he seemed to brighten her life somehow with a genial influence.

'You must have been obliged to think at Oxford,' she said.

Francis Greenwood had taken honours at Oxford a year or so before.

'Not the least in the world. One's tutor does that sort of thing for one. I used to read with a man—a duodecimo edition of Porson in his way, drank like a fish and knew no end of Greek. When I came to a stiffish passage in Aristotle, I used to throw myself back in a chair and light my cigar. "Just help yourself to another s.-and-b., and be good enough to demonstrate that proposition, old fellow, for I don't seem to see it," I used to say; and the dear old bloke would prose away for half an hour, and if I didn't understand it after that, I threw my book at his head and gave it up.'

'Was s.-and-b. a dictionary?' Christabel asked naïvely.

'No, Miss Champion, but a wonderful enlightener of the human understanding—soda-water and brandy.'

'I'm afraid you led quite a dreadful life at the University.'

'Not at all, it was very nice. I should hardly mind leading it over again, only it was not so nice as—'

'As what?' Christabel asked, when he came to a dead stop.

'As the life I hope to lead by and by.'

Her heart sank all at once. That meant his life in the big ugly house that he was to build for himself, and in which he was to set up as a country squire, enriched with the wealth of Perkington and Tanberry. Christabel knew that he was an ardent lover of field-sports, and all pursuits that country gentlemen affect, and that he had a vast capacity for spending money. What more natural than that he should be tempted by Miss Perkington's half-million or so?

She was silent. They had one wide meadow to cross, a meadow where the newly-cut grass was fragrant in the still June air, and they would be in the grounds of the new Hall—grounds in which there were very few trees, but a great deal of ornamentation in the way of costly shrubs of divers spikey orders, and winding gravel paths that were kept with rigorous care. They could hear the sharp clink of the croquet-balls as they crossed the meadow, and shrill feminine laughter.

'It was very rude of you to leave your side so long,' said Christabel.

'My side? O, to be sure, those everlasting croquet-players. Do you know, I think croquet the most duffing—I beg your pardon, the most uninteresting game in the world. A man plays it for the sake of loafing with a girl he likes; I can't see any other attraction in it.'

'I suppose you have been loafing with Miss Perkington,' said Christabel, with a forced little laugh.

Frank Greenwood looked at her curiously.

'Yes.' he answered coolly, 'I have been loafing

with Miss Perkington a good deal lately;' and then he looked at her again.

They were at the iron gate by this time—only a light iron fence divided the grounds from the meadow. Between the lawn and the fence there was that part of the garden called, *par excellence,* a shrubbery—a scanty grove of the spikey tribe, and young pink hawthorn-trees, as thick in the trunk as a *gandin's* umbrella, and guelder-roses dotted about at intervals—a shrubbery in which there was not covert for a rabbit. Christabel felt that the eyes of all the players on the croquet-ground were upon her, as she traversed the meandering gravel walks with Frank by her side.

The lawn was as smooth and as level as a billiard-table, and there was not so much as a faded leaf among the flower-beds—brilliant pyramids of bloom, rising tier upon tier in rings of contrasting colour, or waving in and out in ribbon bordering. The croquet-ground lay on one side of the house, and scattered around it there were iron seats and tables for the accommodation of loungers and lookers-on. Samuel Greenwood was sitting here, smoking his after-dinner cigar, and reading the *Times;*—a big bald-headed man, who might once have been like Frank.

He did not look particularly pleased when Christabel came to shake hands with him, smiling shyly, and he gave his son a side-glance which was not altogether agreeable.

'O, how d'ye do, Miss Champion?' he said. 'I didn't know you were to be here this evening.'

'Good gracious me, pa!' exclaimed the irreverent Rosa, 'as if we should take the trouble to tell you who was coming to play croquet. Come, Chris, you're to be on our side—Harry and I' (short for Harriet), 'Julia Lee' (the rector's daughter), 'and you; Miss Perkington, Frank, Clara Lee, and Patty, on the other side. Now then, first red, get on—O, I forgot to introduce you two girls. Miss Perkington, Miss Champion; Miss Champion, Miss Perkington; aristocracy and plutocracy, Old Rudderford Hall and the Beeches, Leamington; and now you know all about each other, and I expect you to be good friends immediately.'

Miss Perkington bowed stiffly. She did not quite relish such a free-and-easy introduction, but her dear Rosa had such eccentric ways. She was a tall thin young woman, of an order that is called stylish, with a good many sharp angles, which were artfully toned down by the flouncings and puffings of a French dressmaker; a young woman with a complexion of the kind that is vulgarly called 'tallowy,' cold gray eyes, a short nondescript nose, and a heavy lower jaw. She had good white teeth, a profusion of black hair, and she held herself well; but it took a large amount of millinery to make Victoria Perkington attractive.

It was not altogether pleasant to Christabel, that game at croquet. In all their previous sport she had had Frank always on her side, achieving wonders by combined dexterity and dishonesty, now boldly pushing her ball to a point of vantage with the toe of his boot, anon calmly pocketing it to avoid the perils of an adversary's croquet; and they had had such fun, such perpetual giggling, such little secrets and mutual iniquities. This evening they played a rigorous game, Miss Perkington belonged to a croquet-club at Leamington, and would stand no nonsense. She played two hours every afternoon throughout the croquet season, just as regularly as she practised Czerny's exercises on the piano two hours every morning. She had a stroke like a sledgehammer, and never missed a hoop; so she very soon became a rover, and in that capacity kept a sharp eye upon her ally Mr. Francis Greenwood. He had not the smallest opportunity for talking to Christabel, even if he had wished to do so, and poor Christabel fancied that he did not wish. He seemed to be upon quite confidential terms with Miss Perkington. He was in fact a young man who could hardly help making himself agreeable to women, and had that semi-flirting manner which some young men cultivate.

Miss Champion played abominably; suffered herself to be croqueted off the face of the earth, as it were, to the extreme indignation of Rosa Greenwood. The Perkington side won with flying colours. O, how poor Christabel hated the eau-de-Nil dress, with its innumerable flounces and frillings, the point-lace collar, the Cluny borderings, and all the Perkington caparisons, as that sole daughter of the house of Perkington and Tanberry kept rustling to and fro, sending adverse balls to the farthest limits of space with a cold-blooded ferocity that set Miss Champion's teeth on edge!

When the second game had finished, with dire defeat for Christabel's party, and it was about as dark as ever it is at midsummer, with the stars shining out one by one from a deep blue sky, Rosa and one of those useful rectory girls went into the drawing-room, and played the famous 'Mabel' waltzes. The piano had been wheeled into the bay, and the music floated out through the three tall windows, open from floor to ceiling.

Two of the girls waltzed together, and Frank was still Victoria Perkington's partner. He had scarcely asked her to dance: she had appropriated him as a matter of course.

'If I *am* to dance, I suppose it is to be with you,' she said, with her little supercilious laugh, 'since you are our only *danseur*.'

She waltzed very well, with all her canvas spread; waltzed too well, Francis Greenwood thought, for he was waiting for her to be done up, in order that he might get just a turn or so with Christabel. She gave him no opportunity for this, however, as she contrived to hold him in conversation—*fade* society talk about people they both knew at Leamington; but O, it sounded so confidential, so tender even, to Christabel's listening ears!—during the pauses in which Miss Perkington condescended to rest, and then went off again like a steam-engine refreshed.

When Frank did at last make his escape, and cross the lawn in quest of Christabel, a shrill voice from the bay window called out 'Supper!' and he was obliged to abandon all hope of that longed-for waltz.

He offered Miss Champion one arm, and gave the other to one of the rectory girls. These were visitors for the evening, and Miss Perkington was staying in the house, and was, in a manner, a member of the family. The fair Victoria rewarded him with a very black look, notwithstanding, when they all came crowding into the brilliantly-lighted dining-room, where Samuel Greenwood sat at the head of his table with an Aberdeen salmon *a la mayonnaise* before him, a huge silvery fish lying in a bed of greenery, with a bristling bodyguard of prawns.

'Come here, Victoria, my dear,' he said, pointing to the chair on his right; 'Frank, you'll sit next to Miss Perkington; Miss Lee, you come on my left.'

He took no notice of Christabel; but that contumacious Frank put her coolly into the chair next his own, and so seated himself between Miss Perkington and her rival.

The heiress of Perkington and Tanberry retired into herself. Frank tried to divide his attentions between the two girls; but Miss Perkington only answered him with icy monosyllables, and pretended to consider all his attempts at general conversation directed *solely* to Christabel. She scarcely touched her salmon, declined lobster-salad, would have nothing to say to cold chicken or pine-apple cream, left the moselle to waste its fragrance on the desert air, and sat trifling moodily with half-a-dozen monster strawberries.

Her ill-temper seemed to communicate itself to Mr. Greenwood senior, who looked daggers at his son from time to time. The other girls were uneasy. Christabel, who had brightened and sparkled into new life at the beginning of the feast, found out suddenly, in the midst of an animated little discussion, that she and Frank were the only talkers, and grew silent immediately.

The great ormolu and malachite clock upon the chimneypiece struck the halfhour after ten.

'O, if you please,' she whispered to Frank, 'I ought to go away directly, if Mr. Greenwood would not think me rude. David was to come for me at half-past ten—the gardener, you know—and papa might be angry if I were to stop later.'

'David is a nuisance,' said Frank in his free-and-easy manner; 'though our society is not so entertaining that you need regret leaving it. I shall see you home, of course.'

'O no, pray don't think of that; there's really no occasion.'

'There is occasion. You might meet a gang of poachers poaching eggs, or something, and what would David be among so many? There's that fellow they call black Simeon—the man who got seven years for a burglary at Little Thorpington—has come back to Rudderford. I saw him prowling about the village yesterday, half seas-over. A regular bad lot, that fellow is. Of course I shall come with you. David can walk behind and contemplate the stars. I daresay he knows Orion and the Pleiades as well as that fellow in *Locksley Hall*, whose knowledge of the heavenly bodies doesn't seem to have been stupendous.'

The advent of the indoor man from the Rectory, to fetch the Miss Lees, was announced at this moment, so the girls all rose together. A maid who had spirited away Christabel's hat brought it back; and after a very cool good-night from Samuel Greenwood, who sat scowling at the mutilated salmon, and the stiffest possible bow from Miss Perkington, Miss Champion departed, with Frank for her escort.

'Miss Champion has a servant, I believe, Frank,' Mr. Greenwood said sternly.

'I know she has,' answered his undutiful son; 'but I'm going to see her safe across the meadows, for all that.'

Oxford was always too much for Birmingham in any encounter between those two. The commercial magnate had spent three or four thousand pounds upon his son's education, and it seemed to him at odd times that the only tangible produce of that investment was an extensive vocabulary of university slang, and an agreeable placidity of manner which set paternal authority at naught. The young man was not altogether an undutiful son, however, and owned occasionally that his father wasn't 'half a bad fellow.'

CHAPTER IV.

THE moon had risen while they were losing the calm sweetness of the night in the gaslit dining-room; the bright full summer moon had risen, and all the spikey trees in the shrubbery were reflected on the smooth grass as if on water, all the flowers in the garden were breathing perfume. Frank and Christabel went out by the drawing-room window, and forgot all about David, who came running after them by and by from the servants' hall, where he had been regaled with beer, and questioned artfully about the 'queer ways' of his master. He had to come round by back ways and obscure paths, the gardens being sacred from such vulgar feet as his, and thus did not overtake those two till they were half across the first meadow. And yet they had dawdled a good deal in the garden, Frank insisting upon picking an especial yellow rose from a standard of his own planting for Christabel.

'You must have one; roses always smell sweeter picked by moonlight,' he said. 'If you don't find the fact stated in Linnæus, it isn't my fault.'

David was a judicious young man. He followed at a respectful distance, and, as Frank had suggested, contemplated, or seemed to contemplate, the sidereal heavens, chewing a twig of hawthorn thoughtfully the while. He allowed an ample margin for loitering at gates; gave Frank so much latitude, in fact, that before they came to the thick wood which made a darkness round Old Rudderford Hall, that undutiful son had asked Christabel to be his wife. Of course, he had set out with no such intention; but the moonlight, and the dewy meadows fragrant with new-mown hay, and that judicious David, and a tender sweetness in Christabel's blue eyes, had been too much for him, and the words had come of their own accord somehow, he hardly knew how.

Was he sorry when she looked up at him with those sweet eyes brimming over with happy tears, and murmured shyly,

'I thought you were going to marry Miss Perkington!'

'Not for millions of millions, darling!' he cried, not sorry, but rapturously glad, clasping the slender figure to his breast, raining down kisses on the fair young face.

David drew near at this juncture, still intent upon astronomical study, but with the air of thinking he might be wanted presently.

Frank took the hint, released the trembling girl, quite confounded by surprise and joy, and put a little hand through his arm with the calmest air of appropriation.

'It's all settled, darling,' he said; 'I shall call upon your father to-morrow.'

'O Mr. Greenwood!'

'Mr. Greenwood! If you say that again, I shall kiss you again, in spite of David.'

'Frank, then.'

How sweet it was to say it! how sweet it was to hear it!—sweetness known to youth only, that loves and is beloved for the first time. After six or seven such experiences, that sort of thing is apt to become commonplace. It is like one's first watch, one's first Derby-day, one's first whitebait dinner.

'I'm sure your father will never let you marry me, Frank,' said Christabel.

'I should like to see myself asking my governor's permission,' replied the young man. 'He ought to be proud of my getting such a chance—marrying a girl of a grand old family like yours; Brummagem allying itself to the Middle Ages; counting-house getting a leaf in Burke's *County Families*.'

'But we are so poor,' remonstrated Christabel. 'At least—'

'A lift in the social scale is better than money, my dearest. I can take out letters-patent and call myself Greenwood-Champion by and by. That would look rather nice upon our pasteboards, wouldn't it, Belle?'

They were in the deep shadow of the trees by this time. Not a glimmer of light was visible in the old house. All the lower windows were closely guarded by heavy oak shutters. They went to a little door—not the principal entrance, but a low arched door in a side tower—and David rang a bell, which made a tremendous clanging half-a-mile away, as it seemed. They had to wait a considerable time before any one answered this summons, very much to Frank's satisfaction. He was whispering schemes about their future life into Christabel's ear, just as if they had been engaged a twelvemonth; while David looked up at the dark ivy-covered walls, as if calculating the sparrows' nests.

Some one came at last—much too soon for Francis Greenwood. Slipshod feet shuffled along a stone passage, uncertain hands fumbled with locks and bolts, and the door being opened cautiously, revealed the ancient butler in a semi-somnambulistic condition.

'Lard, but you be late, Miss Chrissy,' he said—he had helped to nurse her in her motherless babyhood. 'Your pa's gone to bed ever so long.'

'I'm glad of that,' Christabel whispered to her lover.

'Why, sweetest?'

'Because I never *could* have told him; and if he had seen my face, he might have found out—'

'He shall hear all about it to-morrow, darling. I shall call at one o'clock.'

'And I shall ride Gilpin away to the other end of the world. I couldn't bear to be in the house while —while—'

'While I am in the dock,' said the young man, laughing. 'I think the verdict will be a favourable one, Chrissy.'

'O, you don't know,' cried Christabel dolefully.

'I don't know what, dear?'

'How prejudiced papa is against **your** family,

because of the new Hall being built upon land that once belonged to this, and the estate having been cut up and spoiled so, to make your grounds. Those meadows of yours were a part of our park once.'

'That isn't our fault, darling, but that improvident old Champion's. Who knows but what the two estates might be joined somehow one of these days? My father could buy himself another place; and we'd cut off the new Hall with the smallest possible allowance of garden, and restore this dear old barn'—so lightly did young Oxford speak of a perfect specimen of Tudor architecture—'to its original splendour.'

The sleepy butler coughed faintly, as if to remind them of his infirmities and the lateness of the hour. It was nearly midnight by this time—that walk across the fields had lasted so long. The lovers clasped hands, and said good-night; and Frank would fain have made his last good-night a long business, only there was the butler with his guttering tallow candle and his piteous expostulating look, and David in the rear yawning audibly. So with one warm pressure of the little hand he let her go, and the stout old door closed upon her, like the jaws of a monster that had just swallowed her up.

Francis Greenwood turned away with a sigh, putting his hand in his waistcoat-pocket mechanically to give David baksheesh. But David had vanished, and the courtyard was empty. He looked about meditatively, in no humour to go back to the common world just yet. The wind was sighing faintly among the ivy-leaves, with a sound scarce louder than the breathing of a quiet sleeper; the black wall of the old house rose high above him, the shadow of it fell upon him like a pall.

'What a dismal place for my pet to live in!' he said to himself, and then began to wonder which was her room, and to watch for the glimmer of a light from one of those upper casements.

It came presently; a feeble twinkle, which flitted along a corridor, shining faintly from a row of narrow windows, and then stopped and grew steady in a window at the end of the house. This was his darling's chamber, the young man thought rapturously. It might have been the butler's, but fortunately was not; that functionary, who might have had his pick of twenty vacant rooms, preferring to inhabit a darksome den in the steep sloping roof, where he burrowed like a rabbit. It really was Christabel's room.

Rudderford church clock struck twelve while the lover still stood gazing, and at that very moment, as if conjured into being by the last stroke of the mystic hour, the figure of a man came suddenly from behind an angle of the wall.

'Who the deuce are you?' cried Frank, darting forward.

But the figure had vanished. There was a labyrinth of outbuildings on that side of the house. Frank followed, and prowled round about them, peering into every corner, but could find no trace of that midnight intruder. There is always a nook into which that sort of gentry can screw itself. His search was so close and thorough, that he began at last to fancy his own senses must have deceived him, and that the figure had been only a creature of the imagination. He was not easily satisfied, however. The jewel in that old Tudor casket was to his mind so rare a gem, that no care or watchfulness could be too much in him, whose privilege it was to guard it. He made a complete circuit of the house, trying windows and shutters. On the lower story all was secure as the casements of a beleaguered fortress, close guarded from the foe. If Anthony Champion had been the owner of hoarded millions, he could scarcely have protected himself better from possible burglars.

One o'clock struck before Frank Greenwood left the precincts of the old Hall, and walked slowly away towards the meadows.

CHAPTER V.

CHRISTABEL was almost too happy after that midnight parting. There was no depressing influence to-night in the gloom and silence of her ancient home. All the burden of her loneliness, which she had borne so meekly, was lifted away in a moment, and her future life lay radiant before her, like a garden in fairyland. She was a little anxious about her father, and his strong prejudices against the race of Greenwood; but her lover appeared to her altogether so fascinating and irresistible, that she could not imagine anybody proof against his influence. Her father would like and admire him, of course, just as she did, and would abandon all his prejudices, and accept him as her lover. And Miss Perkington; Christabel laughed aloud — a little happy laugh that startled the silence of the old room — at the thought of that young lady's ignominious defeat; all the silk flounces and lace frillings counting for nothing in the eyes of true love.

She was much too happy to think of sleep for ever so long, although it was past midnight, but paced the room with her hands clasped in a joyous reverie, thinking of the wondrous fortune that had befallen her. Only a retired manufacturer's son, it is true; but then she loved him, and he seemed to her the one most perfect creature in all the world— so bright, so generous, so brave, so true. She had known so few people, had lived a life so utterly lonely, that it is scarcely strange she should believe in the one sunny-natured young fellow who had praised and loved her.

Here she stopped before the tall narrow old glass, and looked at herself half wonderingly.

Was she really pretty? was she worthy of such a lover? She shook out her long loose hair. Yes; she was like a picture of Patient Grisel she remembered seeing years ago in a famous collection.

The clock struck one before she lay down; and then, overcome suddenly by sleep in the midst of her happy thoughts, she threw herself down, dressed as she was, upon a sofa, to rest a little before going seriously to bed; and thereupon fell into a deep slumber, which seemed likely to last all night.

She had one bad habit, engendered perhaps of

long lonely days, with much time for thoughtfulness and waking dreams—the habit of walking in her sleep. It was not a thing that happened to her often, but once in a way—two or three times in a year, perhaps, when her mind had been in any way disturbed during the day—she had been wont to wander. The servants had met her at daybreak, sometimes, in the corridor, or out on the broad square landing beyond, or on the stairs even, descending ghostlike, with open unseeing eyes. One luckless country lass, taking her for the ghost of that slaughtered lady whose spirit was reported to haunt the Hall, had fled shrieking to the kitchen, where she fell into violent hysterics, clutching the air, and well-nigh strangling herself with her sobs and screams.

And so it happened to-night. Towards three o'clock, just as the moon was waning, the girl rose from her sofa, pushed open the door which she had left ajar, and went out into the corridor—a tall white figure faintly visible in the dim light.

She went straight on to an angle of the corridor where there was a narrow window cut in a part of the wall where the ivy grew thickest. As she came slowly forward, this window was opened by a stealthy hand,

and a man thrust his head and shoulders through the window.

He was on the point of leaping through, when his eyes—evil eyes they were, too—fell upon that mysterious figure, with the white dress and loose flowing hair, the figure he had heard of many a time, when folks talked of the ghost that haunted Old Rudderford Hall.

He dropped his stick with an ejaculation. The fall of the jagged stake, cut from a hedge and trimmed with a rough hasty hand, upon the uncarpeted oak floor, awakened Christabel. She gave a loud shriek, and stared at the intruder transfixed. That shriek was alarming enough; but it reassured him. He sprang into the corridor, and clapped his great horny hand upon her mouth.

'What, it's you, is it?' he exclaimed in a cautious voice. 'Hold your row; or I shall have to quiet you with my clasp-knife. What brings you prowling about at this time of night, I wonder? After that chap that was prowling outside about an hour ago, I suppose. Come, young lady, you just walk into your own room, and keep yourself to yourself; I've got business to do here.'

He had tied a big bird's-eye handkerchief across

the girl's mouth—she was not fully awake yet, and had only a confused sense of peril and horror—and had just produced another, with a view to tying it round her wrists, when a great crash of glass sounded close behind him, and Frank Greenwood sprang through the open window, smashing the casement as he came through.

Love is so foolish, so full of morbid doubts and apprehensions. He had come back to the old Hall, after crossing the meadows on his way home, not able to feel comfortable about that lurking figure which he had seen at midnight, and had come back just in time to rescue his betrothed from the clutch of a ruffian, and to save the Champion diamonds,—a very valuable portion of his future wife's dowry.

The man was Black Simeon the poacher. He had been lurking about the night before, when Mr. Champion showed his daughter the family jewels, had seen the gems and where they were kept, and had hidden himself in the shrubbery when Christabel came out to reconnoitre. To-night he had tried all the lower doors and windows, and finding entrance below impossible, had clambered up the ivy to this casement at the end of the corridor, trusting to his good luck to grope his way down-stairs to the library.

The intent but not the deed confounded him. He was pinioned and locked in an empty wine-cellar that night, and handed over to the local authorities at breakfast-time, to appear by and by, charged with a burglarious attempt, and to return to that state of bondage from which he had so lately emerged.

Anthony Champion could hardly be uncivil to the man who had saved his daughter and the family diamonds; and Frank Greenwood really was a nice young fellow, with free-and-easy irresistible ways. He brought brightness and life into the gloomy old house, and in an incredibly short time persuaded the master of Old Rudderford Hall to waive his prejudices against the inmates of New Rudderford Hall.

When he had smoothed the way by his artful management, he coolly ordered his father to call upon Mr. Champion, to entreat that gentleman's consent to the union of the two houses. The manufacturer was furious, and there was a scene; but a very brief one. Frank's supreme coolness made light of everything. Miss Perkington had departed before this in silent disgust, with all her baggage. Samuel Greenwood was fain to give way; it evidently mattered so very little to his son whether he did or not.

'I can always make a living at the Bar,' said

young Oxford, in his careless way, 'and there's the five hundred a year my poor mother left me. I should like to have made an amicable arrangement, and secured your coöperation for restoring the old Hall; but if it isn't to be, why it isn't; you know best; and we sha'n't starve.'

Samuel fretted and fumed, swore an oath or two, and succumbed. He went to call upon Mr. Champion with lamb-like meekness, and returned crestfallen.

Mr. Champion was prepared to waive all consideration of the wide difference between the status of the two families, and to consent to the marriage. He could give his daughter fifty thousand pounds, and jewels worth at least twenty-five thousand more. Mr. Greenwood had supposed him to be a pauper.

'It has been my fancy to live like this,' he said, 'and allow the surplus of my income to accumulate for my only child.'

And so they were married, and were just the sort of couple to live happily ever afterwards.

THE SPLENDID STRANGER

THIRTY years ago there were still stage-coaches between London and Lowminster; and in the early dusk of spring and autumn, in the misty darkness of winter, and in the rosy western sunshine of summer-time, the music of the guard's horn and the rattle of the wheels used to sound cheerily in the sleepy rural street, where the upper stories of the quaint old houses projected over the narrow pavement, and where there were more steeply-sloping roofs, narrow-peaked gables, and diamond-paned casements than in any other town in Midlandshire. In those days the modern builder had done nothing to disturb the pleasant air of antiquity that pervaded the High-street, and harmonised well with the gray old gothic cross in the Market-place, and the splendid gloom of the Cathedral—a noble pile which lay a little way off the town, and was surrounded by half-a-dozen low rambling dwelling-houses, with queerly-shaped old gardens shut-in from the outer world by walls so ponderously built, that the brick in their many buttresses would have served for the building of a whole terrace of modern houses. These curious and spacious habitations belonged, for the most part, to the ecclesiastical dignitaries of the place, whose quiet existence was chiefly spent under the shadow of the old cathedral, and who were regarded as a superior race of beings by the humbler towns-folk. Altogether Lowminster was a comfortable well-to-do kind of a place; and for the weary wayfarer who came thither from the press and turmoil of busier scenes, the sleepy out-of-the-world air of the old cathedral town was apt to have a soothing influence as refreshing as the cool breath of ocean breezes to the wanderer from a sandy desert. Beyond the town there were low fertile meadows and winding trout-streams, narrow lanes where the hedges grew high and wild, and where there was a wealth of dog-roses and honeysuckle in the summer-time; and here and there a gray ivy-grown old farm-house, or a water-mill with the miller's comfortable cottage nestling beside it, came suddenly upon the pedestrian, inspiring him with the fancy that life must be pleasant and peaceful in these out-of-the-way nooks, and that time must here glide softly by in unison with the murmur of the dripping water, and the far-away sound of the cathedral bells, like a poem set to solemn music.

There was one particular miller who lived a very little way out of the town, at the end of a rustic lane behind the cathedral—a lane that was just broad enough for his wagons, but in which two vehicles could not pass each other without damage to one of the hedges. The cottage was one of the prettiest in the neighbourhood of Lowminster, a low white building, with a good deal of ponderous timber about it painted black, and with roses and honeysuckle growing almost as high as the chimneys. There was a rustic porch covered with jasmine and clematis, and opening straight into the every-day sitting-room; and there were long low diamond-paned casements, with broad ledges, on which were always jars of flowers.

Close beside the cottage flowed a broad deep stream, quite a young river in its way, in which the great mill-wheel went slowly round with a creaking noise in the still summer mornings. Farther off in the meadows through which it took its winding way this stream was renowned for trout, and Mr. Baxter was in the habit of letting a parlour and bedroom occasionally to any gentlemanly angler who came that way. The house was too large for the requirements of John Baxter and his two daughters, and the miller was not rich enough to be indifferent to any small profit that might be made in this manner.

One midsummer morning full thirty years ago a gentleman came to the cottage with his rod upon his shoulder, and asked to see the rooms that were to let. It was a sultry drowsy kind of morning, and he found Mary Baxter, the miller's younger daughter, leaning over the rustic wooden gate, looking dreamily out across the meadows, with her pretty blue eyes.

She looked up with a bright startled glance as the stranger approached, and he thought he had never seen a fairer face.

'This is Mr. Baxter's house, I believe?' he said.

'Yes, sir; my father's name is Baxter. Did you please to want him?'

'The people at the coach-office told me that I could get lodgings here. I have come to Lowminster for a few weeks' fishing and change of air; rather more for the sake of the country air than the sport, in fact, as I have been very ill.'

Mary Baxter glanced at him with a gentle sympathising look as she offered to show him the rooms. He was very handsome—the handsomest man she had ever seen; but there was a haggard worn look about his face, and his black eyes had a melancholy look, Mary thought, as of a man with whom life had gone wrong. He was not in his first youth — was about five-and-thirty, perhaps — and he had a kind of weary air, as if he had outlived all the pleasures and hopes of youth, and had nothing to expect in the future.

'Yes, the rooms will do very well,' he said carelessly; and then asked the terms in so indifferent a tone, that Mary fancied money could be of no importance to him.

He agreed to pay the price she named without the faintest objection; and then walked listlessly round the garden with Mary and looked at the stream, about which he showed the nearest approach to interest that he had yet displayed upon any subject.

'It is all very pretty and rustic,' he said. 'I'll go back to the coach-office, and tell them to send my portmanteau.'

'Shall I send one of the boys from the mill, sir?' asked Mary. 'You may be tired, being an invalid as you say, sir.'

'It is very good of you to be so considerate. No,

I am not tired; I should rather like the walk.' He lifted his hat to her at the little garden-gate, and then went away with his slow lounging step through the sultry noontide. Mary watched him thoughtfully.

'Poor fellow!' she muttered to herself softly; 'what a melancholy expression he has! He seems to have suffered from some great sorrow.'

The gentleman she pitied thus had indeed suffered from great sorrow, chiefly connected with an obstinate run of ill-luck at cards, and an unfortunate selection of horses for the Derby and other great racing events; but Mary, who was a tender romantic little creature, fancied that his griefs must lie nearer the heart. He had loved, perhaps, and had loved in vain, though that seemed almost impossible for one so gifted; or, more likely, the object of his affections had died on the eve of her wedding-day—Mary had read of such things in books. Some melancholy romance, she was convinced, was attached to the stranger with the pale handsome face and deep dark eyes.

She stood at the gate for some minutes, meditating thus, and then ran off to the mill, to tell her father that the lodgings were let. When she went back to the house, she found her sister Harriet, who had just returned from a morning's marketing and gossip in Lowminster; and the two girls set to work to prepare the rooms for the stranger, assisted by a trim little maid-servant. Mary ran out into the garden to gather fresh roses; and the little sitting-room was perfumed with their rich odour when the stranger arrived by and by, followed by a lad carrying a large black-leather portmanteau.

He took no notice of the roses, though they were the finest Mary had been able to find in the garden; and he asked the sisters, in rather a peevish tone, what they could give him for dinner. Mary was a little disappointed to find him so much interested in the dinner question; but then he was an invalid, she argued with herself, and invalids are apt to attach undue importance to such things. Harriet, who was a thorough housekeeper, and had no romantic aversion to the dinner question, suggested an excellent bill of fare; and this matter being settled to the satisfaction of the new lodger, the two girls retired, Mary to the sunny parlour, where she sat down to her needlework by the open window; Harriet to the kitchen, to superintend and assist the preparation of the new lodger's dinner.

Mary had plenty of time to think of the stranger's melancholy face as she sat at work all through the drowsy summer afternoon, with a great bee buzzing and booming and bumping himself violently against the diamond-paned casement, and with the perfume of a thousand flowers floating in upon her from the fertile garden. Yes, he was very handsome, there could be no doubt of that; and there was something strangely interesting in his haggard careworn face. If he had been in robust health and high spirits, she would have thought very little about him, she fancied; but there was a kind of mystery in that troubled look of his which could not fail to interest every one. She talked him over with her sister presently, when Harriet came in from the kitchen, and was surprised to find how little curiosity he had inspired in that eminently practical mind. Harriet owned that he was handsome, and remarked that his clothes were of the very best material, and seemed to be made in a more fashionable and elegant style than was common to the gentlemen of Lowminster.

'He is in the army, I suppose,' said Miss Baxter in conclusion; 'I saw a brass plate on his portmanteau, with "Captain Herriston" upon it.'

'Herriston!' repeated Mary. 'What a pretty name!'

It seemed to her a very pretty name, as everything about the stranger seemed to her elegant and attractive. She saw him strolling in the garden by and by as she sat at her work; and he came to the window, and talked to her with a manner that was listless in spite of his politeness, yet which seemed to Mary Baxter the most perfect manner in the world. She was only nineteen, and this splendid stranger was the first interesting person she had ever encountered. It was scarcely strange if he appeared to her to belong to a different race of beings from the young men of Lowminster—the smart, well-to-do, over-dressed tradesmen's sons who admired her and paid her compliments in their clumsy manner, when she and her sister met them in the meadows after the Sunday-afternoon service at the cathedral.

Captain Herriston talked very little, but he stood a long time by the window, dropping out a lazy sentence now and then. In the evening Mr. Baxter smoked his pipe in a rustic arbour at the end of the garden, according to his custom in this summer weather; and while he was sitting there with his two daughters, Captain Herriston came out and joined the family group, pleased to find that he might smoke his cigar in the presence of the young ladies. He quite drew the miller out in a conversational way by his questions about Lowminster, Mr. Baxter dilating much upon the prosperity of the sleepy old place, and the fortunes that some of the leading tradespeople had made in it.

'Why, there's Josiah Greenock—you might have noticed his shop, perhaps, as you drove by—fishmonger and poulterer; if that man is worth sixpence, he's worth a plum; and there's Martin the butcher pretty nigh as rich, I daresay. Esther Greenock and my daughter Mary are uncommon fond of each other—they were at school together; but Harriet, you see, she stopped at home to take care of me, and I don't think there's a better housekeeper in Midlandshire. A very nice girl is Esther Greenock; a little set-up, perhaps, on account of her father's money, but a very nice girl for all that, and like a sister to my Mary.—I haven't seen you two together lately, by-the-bye, Molly,' he added, turning to his daughter. 'What's come of Esther?'

'She's staying at Woodgreen with her aunt, father,' answered Mary; 'she's likely to be away the best part of the summer.'

'You haven't been whipping the stream down yonder yet, sir?' asked the miller presently.

'No, Mr. Baxter,' answered Captain Herriston. 'To tell you the truth, though I carry a rod and tackle, I am no very enthusiastic angler. I have come to Lowminster more with a view to the recovery of my health than for the sake of the fishing; but of course I shall try my luck. It will be an easy way of getting rid of my time, for one thing.'

He gave a short impatient sigh as he said this, and walked away from the arbour after wishing its inmates a brief good-night. When they came to know him better by and by, they found that he was subject to these sudden changes of mood.

He stayed at the miller's cottage for many weeks, whipping the stream daily without any very profitable result in the way of fish; and dawdling away his evenings in the garden, sometimes smoking his cigar in the arbour, sometimes strolling among the flower-beds or under the old apple-trees in the orchard with the two girls, or with one of them— more often with one of them, and that one was Mary.

He had grown very confidential in his talk with her before many weeks were over, while the roses were still blooming in the pretty rustic garden. He told her all his troubles, rambling on about himself in a gloomy discontented way, which seemed to afford a kind of relief to his mind. Yes, there had been troubles of the heart, as well as money difficulties. He told her how he had been engaged to a very charming girl with a large fortune, and how the lady's father had interposed in a most infamous manner to prevent the match. Everything in life seemed to have gone wrong with him. His own father had treated him badly. He had been obliged to sell-out of the army, for reasons which he described rather vaguely to Mary Baxter; and he had come down to Lowminster thoroughly weary of his existence. Prospects he had none. He was the poorest, most miserable castaway that ever cumbered the earth.

Mary was never tired of listening to these complaints, and of pitying Captain Herriston's afflictions. In all his troubles he had never come to neglect his appearance. His dress was always perfection, even in that retired life; his whiskers faultless. From the gold-and-onyx studs which fastened his wristbands to the turquoise pin in his cravat, everything that he wore was alike elegant and costly.

His dressing-case seemed to Mary the most beautiful thing in creation when she peeped shyly into his room, and saw the bright confusion of his table, where there were ivory-backed brushes and glittering bottles of perfume. She asked him once how he could be poor, when he had so many beautiful things belonging to him.

He laughed at her innocence.

'My dear Miss Baxter,' he said, 'a man keeps such things as those to the last. I have money enough to rub on with a little longer, and my creditors must wait. The question is, What am I to do in the future? Choose a new profession, as my friends obligingly suggest? Rather a difficult thing to do when a man has passed his thirtieth birthday. Or emigrate, and turn sheep-farmer? Something must be done. I came down here sick and tired of London life, and in hopes that some brilliant inspiration might seize me in the quiet of the country; but I have been here a good many weeks, and the inspiration has not arrived. No, Mary, upon my soul, I do not know what is to become of me!'

He called her 'Mary' sometimes, in a careless absent-minded way; and the sound of her name, so spoken, always sent a faint thrill through her heart

—a tremulous kind of sensation, half pleasure, half pain.

So they dawdled on until the summer was quite gone, and Captain Herriston gave no sign of departure. He had paid his way regularly enough for the first few weeks, but after that had fallen into arrear. The miller was an easy-going sort of man, and liked his lodger; so when the Captain assured him that the money would be paid early in October, at which date he expected remittances, Mr. Baxter consented to wait. The Captain remained. He wasted a good deal of his time in the meadows, fishing for something or other, though all chance of trout was over; and he contrived somehow to meet Mary Baxter very often in these lonely rambles. Whether they met by concert, no one knew but themselves. The miller was busy all day long, and Harriet's household duties completely absorbed her time and thoughts; so Mary was tolerably free to go where she pleased.

To her those long rambles through the lanes and meadows, and over the grassy hills that made a kind of amphitheatre round Lowminster, were like wanderings in some new garden of Eden. It seemed to her as if a new and wonderful life had opened before her footsteps since she first saw James Herriston's face.

They had been plighted lovers for some time past. He had not been able to resist the shy glances of those tender eyes, which told him so innocently that he was beloved; and one day, when the two were alone together in the garden, the words which sealed Mary Baxter's fate were spoken.

'Mary,' he said to her suddenly, 'upon my life, I believe you love me.'

He looked down at her blushing face with a half-amused smile upon his own.

'Such a worthless, purposeless fellow as I am, too —undeserving any good woman's regard,' he went on, in his slow listless way.

Mary flamed up indignantly at this. He was not worthless. He deserved the love of a much better woman than herself—of any lady in the land.

'My dearest girl,' he said, still smiling down upon her, as if she had been a pretty child, 'what can I give to any woman ? what hope in the future, what position in the present ? You are the sweetest and loveliest girl I ever knew in my life; and if I were not the man I am, I would ask you to marry me to-morrow.'

'If I thought you loved me,' she faltered, 'that is all in the world I should care for.'

'I do love you, Mary; it is impossible to know you as I do, and not love you. If ever I am in a position to marry, you shall be my wife; but Heaven only knows if that day will ever come.'

It was after this that they met so often in the lanes and meadows. Mary was unspeakably happy in the knowledge that James Herriston loved her. She looked forward very vaguely to that remote future in which she might be his wife. It was enough for her to know that she was beloved by this man, who seemed to her as high above her as if he had been some exiled prince. They never talked of the future. James Herriston accepted Mary's homage with a lazy kind of satisfaction. He was happier than he had been for some time in this girl's society. He felt himself, in a manner, rehabilitated by such devoted love. He was not so worthless, after all; he had not quite outlived his power to charm. He smiled at his handsome image in the looking-glass, and sang a few bars of an Italian serenade in his rich deep voice, as he thought of Mary's worship.

'Poor little soul, how she loves me!' he said to himself. 'If I were only a rich man, or if she had money, instead of being a hard-working miller's daughter! Poor little girl! It never can come to anything, of course; but it is pleasant to be loved like that.'

He had begged Mary to say nothing about their attachment to her father or her sister. Under such uncertain circumstances, it was so much better to keep matters to themselves, he urged; and Mary had agreed to this, knowing the practical turn of mind which prevailed in her family, and that neither her father nor her sister would be likely to approve of an engagement in which marriage was such a remote contingency.

So things went on in the pleasant early autumn weather, Captain Herriston growing daily more intimate with the miller's family, and spending all his evenings in their common sitting-room. Honest unsuspicious John Baxter liked him very much, and was delighted with his talk about that outer world of which he himself knew so little.

It was about the middle of September when Esther Greenock came home from her long visit to an aunt who lived in the next county. The rich Mr. Greenock had built himself a handsome house not very far from John Baxter's mill, and it was Esther's habit to spend a great deal of her time with her friend Mary when she was at home. Her return, therefore, in a great measure put a stop to those quiet rambles with Captain Herriston, until Mary obtained her lover's permission to tell Esther of her engagement, of course under the seal of secrecy. After this, the walks went on as before, only that Esther now very often accompanied the lovers, and they seemed all the gayer for her society. She was a clever high-spirited girl, with a very good opinion of herself, founded, perhaps, not a little on the fact that she was sole heiress to her father's large fortune. It was considered in Lowminster that she would most likely make some brilliant match; and Esther was inclined to agree with Lowminster upon this point, though where the bridegroom was to come from remained a profound enigma, only to be solved by time. She was good-looking, in rather a bold common style, dressed in the height of provincial fashion, and strummed upon the piano with more recklessness than skill.

Of course Mary was anxious to know what her friend thought of Captain Herriston. Esther acknowledged that he was handsome, and had agreeable, not to say fascinating, manners; but she was not enthusiastic in her praise of him, and Mary thought her cold. She wanted all the world to bow down before her idol, and she was almost inclined to resent Miss Greenock's cool dismissal of the subject.

Esther seemed, however, by no means to dislike the Captain's company in her walks with her friend. She wore her prettiest bonnets, and put on her most animated manner during these rural rambles. She made her father invite the miller's family to tea and supper, including Captain Herriston; and she played and sang to him in the gaudy newly-furnished drawing-room. Poor Mary looked on rather wistfully during this performance, wishing that she could play the piano, and were more like a lady, for her lover's sake—wishing, above all, that she had Esther Greenock's wealth with which to endow him. For her own part she had no fear of poverty with him. What could be greater happiness than to be his slave, to wait upon him, and toil for him?

She told him so by and by, in answer to some querulous speech of his about 'that old Greenock's money,' as they walked home arm-in-arm a little way behind the others. She told him how happily she could endure poverty for his sake.

'That's all very well, Mary,' he answered, 'and highly flattering to me; but, you see, I can't endure poverty myself, and I will never marry until I can afford to keep a wife decently.'

Mary caught a severe cold soon after this little party, and was in the doctor's care and not allowed to leave her room for some time, during which imprisonment she was much distressed to think of her lover's solitude. She asked Harriet every day how the Captain was employing himself, and heard every day that he was out—he went out early with his fishing-rod, and did not come home till his six o'clock dinner. The weather was unusually fine just then, and there was every temptation for him to be out of doors; but still Mary felt she would rather he had stayed more at home while she was so ill.

'What pleasure should I take in the sunshine if he were ill?' she thought to herself; 'I should not care to stir from the house.'

Esther Greenock came now and then during her friend's illness, but she happened on each occasion to be in a hurry, and Mary fancied that her old cordial manner had given place to a kind of restraint.

It was on a mild sunless day that Mary was allowed to go down-stairs for the first time since her illness. She had been confined to her room nearly a fortnight, and this time, measured by her separation from her lover, had seemed to her very long. She trembled a little as she slowly dressed herself, thinking how soon she was to see him, and wondering what he would say to her, and how he would look as he took her hand for the first time after this dreary severance. Would it be as difficult for him to conceal his agitation as she was sure it would be for her?

Breakfast had been over some time when she went down-stairs. The house was very quiet—unnaturally quiet it seemed to Mary, in her impatience to hear that one voice she loved so well. The door of Captain Herriston's sitting-room was open, and the room was empty. He was out, then, again to-day! The disappointment came upon her with a sudden chill. She had hoped that he would have heard of her coming down-stairs, and would have stopped at home to see her.

Her sister Harriet came in from the garden while the invalid stood for a moment before that open door; —came in looking as fresh and bright and active as if there were no such thing as sorrow in the world.

'Why, Mary,' said she, 'I didn't expect to see you down so soon. I was coming up to help you to dress. Go into the parlour, child; there's a fire in there, lighted on purpose for you. Go in and make yourself

S

warm. You look as pale as a ghost. I think the doctor would send you back to bed if he saw you.'

Mary obeyed her sister, and seated herself by the fireside with a very listless air.

'Captain Herriston has gone out, I suppose?' she said presently.

'Yes; he went very early this morning. He has gone to London for a week.'

'To London?'

'Yes, to London. Why, child, how you stare! Father's money will be all right, he says. He has taken nothing with him but a carpet-bag, and he is to be back in a week.'

For a few minutes Mary Baxter sat quite still, with her hands clasping the arms of the chair, trembling very much and unable to speak. Her sister was too busy with her needlework to observe the girl's agitation.

'It's very sudden, isn't it, Harriet?' she said at last, in a faint voice.

'The Captain's leaving? Yes, he had some letter from London last night, it seems, and he was obliged to go there on business.'

Mary lay back in her chair, with half-closed eyes, for the rest of the morning, thinking drearily of the long dull week that must drag itself to an end before James Herriston's return. Harriet went on quietly with her work, thinking that her sister was enjoying a pleasant doze; until the burly miller came into his dinner, when poor Mary had to rouse herself from that dismal reverie, and receive her father's congratulations upon her recovery.

'You look very white and feeble yet, though, my lass,' he said; 'but it's pleasant to see you downstairs again; and you'll pick up your strength all the faster down here, I daresay.'

She smiled at him faintly, as she stood leaning against him a little, with one slender arm round his neck. In spite of Harriet's usefulness to him, Mary had always been his favourite. The girl knew this, and thought with a remorseful pang of that strange idol which she had worshipped to the neglect of her doating old father. She sat down on a low stool at his feet by and by, when he was smoking his after-dinner pipe, and laid her pretty head upon his knee. The slow tears stole down her pale cheeks as she sat thus, thinking of her absent lover and the sin that she had sinned against her father in concealing the fact of their attachment.

It was a leisure afternoon with the miller; and

when he had finished his pipe, he strolled out to the garden-gate, and stood there with his arms resting on the topmost bar, lazily contemplating the landscape, and waiting for a gossip with any neighbour who might happen to pass that way. He had not long to wait. One of his old cronies came down the lane presently, and stopped at the gate nearly half an hour talking. Mary watched the two men from her chair by the fire, wondering what they were talking about so earnestly—wondering at their cheerfulness too. It seemed strange to her that every one did not feel the dulness of the place now, when its very life and brightness had departed with James Herriston.

John Baxter came back to the parlour by and by rubbing his hands.

'Here's strange news for you, girls,' he said. 'Esther Greenock has run away—disappeared this morning before breakfast, leaving a letter for her father, telling him she was going to be married to the man she loved, and that it was not a bit of use going after her, as she'd made up her mind, and nothing in the world could turn her.'

'Esther going to be married, father?' cried Mary. 'Why, I never knew there was any one she cared for!'

'Nor any one else either, it seems,' answered the miller. 'The man must be some one she got acquainted with while she was away at her aunt's. Old Greenock was in an awful rage, Sam Wills told me just now; but instead of going after his daughter, as every one thought he would, he said she had made her bed, and might lie upon it. He wasn't going to waste time and trouble looking after her. And now it comes out that he's going to marry Joe Ashton's daughter,—you know Ashton, that has got a small farm at Overingham?—and ain't particularly sorry to get rid of Miss Esther, who always rode the high horse with him.'

The miller went out after tea. It was a clubnight at a little tavern in Lowminster—a night when the tradesmen of the place met for a weekly gossip over their clay pipes. John Baxter was one of the steadiest and most sober of men, and it was only a little after nine when he came home from this simple gathering.

'Well, girls,' he said, as he seated himself in his arm-chair by the fire, 'they've found out all about Miss Esther's beau. They went off together at seven o'clock this morning in a postchaise from the Black Lion. You'll never guess who it is.'

Mary rose suddenly from her chair, white to the very lips.

'Captain Herriston,' she said.

'Why, you must have known something about it, surely, lass!' cried the miller. 'That's the man.'

'I thought so,' she said faintly, and sat down again without another word; and went to bed by and by without having betrayed her secret by the smallest sign.

So she bore her trial silently and submissively to the very end. Three days after the elopement, a letter came for John Baxter, enclosing a cheque for the amount of Captain Herriston's debt, and requesting that his portmanteau might be sent to a certain hotel at the West-end. This was all. Three months after this, Mr. Greenock married Sophy Ashton, a pretty girl of about twenty. The Baxters heard about the same time that he had settled three hundred a-year upon his daughter—a very small amount compared with that young lady's expectations; and that Mr. and Mrs. Herriston were living at some small town in France.

No one ever guessed Mary's trouble. She was a long time recovering from that attack of cold and low fever which the doctor had prognosticated would be an affair of a week or two; but she did recover, and went about the house with her old light step once more. Never again with the old gaiety of spirit —that was gone for ever. There was a gentle placidity in her manner which was very beautiful; but she was never again to be the bright happy creature she had been before the advent of James Herriston. No one suspected the cause or the nature of this change. Her friends only remarked that she had grown 'steadier.'

Years went by, and Mary Baxter had more than one eligible offer of marriage from prosperous young tradesmen in Lowminster; but advancing years found both the sisters confirmed old maids. The miller died, and they were obliged to leave the comfortable old house in which their quiet uneventful lives had been spent. They were not well-off by any means after their father's death; so they took a small house on the outskirts of the town, and eked-out their slender income by letting lodgings.

Eight-and-twenty years had gone by since Esther Greenock's elopement. Harriet and Mary Baxter were now two quiet-looking women with iron-gray hair, always dressed in gray or neutral tints, and with a look of settled spinsterhood about them, a genteel faded air, and a most scrupulous neatness and purity in the details of their quaker-like costume. They were happy together in a quiet monotonous way, and loved each other dearly. Things had gone tolerably well with them; for they were liked and respected by all Lowminster, and people were always pleased to do them a good turn. Mr. Greenock's young wife had brought him two bouncing sons, to the ruin of Esther's expectations. She had never received more from her father than the three hundred a-year, and had long ceased to receive that. News of her death had come to Lowminster about ten years after her marriage. She had died at Nice after a lingering illness, and had died childless.

The house in which Harriet and Mary Baxter lived was in a quiet little street on one side of an old arched gateway at the beginning of Lowminster —a gray old gothic arch, beyond which there were only a few straggling villas on the broad high-road. It was a modest little dwelling-place, lying some way back from its neighbours, with a patch of garden before it, where the flowers grew almost as luxuriantly as in the old garden by the mill-stream. The inside of the house was a picture in its neatness and spotlessness, and there was a quaint faded prettiness about everything, and an all-pervading odour of dried rose-leaves and lavender, that had a kind of melancholy charm. All the furniture was old and out of date; but the spindle-legged mahogany tables and brass-handled bureaus shone like so many mirrors, and the roomy old easy-chairs were brightened by cushions with the freshest chintz covers, all rosebuds and apple-blossom.

One cold autumn evening an invalid gentleman came to take the lodgings. He had been recommended by the chemist, he told the two spinster ladies, and he expressed himself much pleased with the rooms they showed him. He was a tall man, with a thick gray beard that concealed all the lower part of his face, gray hair and eyebrows, and very bright black eyes—eyes that gave Mary Baxter a strange puzzled feeling as she looked at them. He told them that his name was Howard, and that he meant to spend the winter at Lowminster.

Everything was settled easily. The stranger agreed to the terms, and took the lodgings from that moment, establishing himself at once before the newly-lighted fire in the pretty little parlour. His luggage was to be sent from the railway station.

Mr. Howard was a very quiet lodger. He used

to rise late, sit all day reading and writing, and stroll out at dusk to smoke a cigar in the shady little street. He seldom walked much farther than this, and seemed indeed to have little strength to spare. He was not a troublesome person by any means, but was self-indulgent, and very particular about what he ate. Harriet made him nice little dishes, and pampered him a good deal in this respect.

He complained sometimes of being very lonely, and would send the old servant-of-all-work to the sisters sometimes of an evening, with his compliments, to ask if he might come to their room for half an hour's chat. The request was always politely answered; and he would come and sit with the two ladies for the greater part of the evening, telling them all the news of the busy world which he had read in the day's paper, and hearing their little humdrum gossip about the people of Lowminster. By and by he proposed a hand at cards; and after this it became an established thing with them to play whist with a dummy every evening.

This lasted for some time, during which he paid his weekly bills with unfailing punctuality; but after seven or eight weeks he began to fall into arrear. His health grew worse, and he was no longer able to write, nor did he care now for the evening rubber of whist. His spirits sank very low with the change in his health, and he entreated the sisters to sit with him of an evening and to bear him company, and in the day too, sometimes.

'I am very low,' he said; 'but I shall be better soon, I daresay. Your money will be all right, Miss Baxter.'

This was to Harriet; he never spoke of money to Mary.

'There is something due to me from a London publisher, which I am sure to receive soon. And I shall be able to write again in a week or so.'

Harriet Baxter shook her head despondently as she told her sister this presently.

'I don't believe he'll ever get any better, or that he'll ever pay us what he owes, Mary,' she said; 'we ought to get rid of him somehow or other.'

'What!' cried Mary, 'turn him out of doors in his weak state? Why, it would be a kind of murder. I wonder you can think of such a thing, Harriet. You so tender-hearted too!'

Harriet wiped her eyes, and kissed her sister.

'Well, my dear,' she answered resignedly, 'I suppose we must make the best of it, and go on trusting him a little longer. But it seems rather hard upon us. The money we saved in the summer will soon go.'

'Never mind, dear; we can save more next summer. Anything is better than to turn that poor creature out of doors.'

Before long, this unprofitable lodger absorbed all their time and care. The Lowminster doctor gave little hope of his recovery. Mary Baxter nursed him night and day, devoting herself to the task with a patience that knew no change. Her sister remonstrated with her sometimes about this constant fatigue, but she would hear of no objection to her doing what she called her duty.

'But it can't be your duty to sacrifice your life for this man, Mary,' said Harriet, 'and he quite a stranger to us too.'

'So was the traveller that the Samaritan took care of, Harriet. You needn't fear my being any the worse for what I do. It would do me more harm to be fidgeting myself about that poor creature, as I should, if I left Anne to take care of him.'

The sick man lingered on through the beginning of the year. The days had lengthened a good deal, and the little garden was full of crocuses, when he began to sink. The money had never come from the London publisher, and he owed the Miss Baxters more than thirty pounds.

He was lying on a sofa near the window one day, in the fading sunshine of a bright afternoon, with Mary Baxter sitting near him at work, when he called her for the first time by her Christian name.

'Mary,' he said, very gently, 'I think you are the truest woman and the best Christian I ever knew. God knows your goodness to me is quite enough to prove you that. Yet there are some injuries which even a Christian finds it hard to forgive. Did any one ever do you such a wrong as that?'

He lifted himself on his elbow, and looked her in the face with a very earnest expression. Her clear blue eyes, which had retained their beauty amidst all the changes time had wrought in the once lovely face, looked full into his.

'No,' she said; 'I have forgiven every wrong that was ever done me.'

'You have forgiven a man who won your love only to throw it away—a man called James Herriston, whose story I learned a long time ago?'

Mary Baxter looked at him with a smile.

'I never cherished any feeling of resentment against James Herriston,' she said gently.

'And yet he injured you deeply?'

'He broke my heart.'

'Mary!'

'O, I daresay that seems hard to believe, because I went on living; but a broken heart does not always kill.'

The sick man fell back upon his pillow with a long-drawn sigh. He shaded his face with one thin hand, and lay thus for some minutes silent, while Mary quietly resumed her work. By and by he raised himself again upon his arm.

'Come here, Mary,' he said.

She went to him, and knelt down beside the sofa.

'Look at me, my dear, and tell me if there is anything in my face that reminds you of the past.'

She looked at him for a few moments in silence, with the same quiet smile upon her face.

'O James Herriston,' she said at last; 'did you think you could deceive me? I knew you from the first day you came here.'

'And you have done so much for me, and been so good to me, knowing I was the wretch who jilted you thirty years ago? O Mary, what generous creatures women are! There is no limit to the goodness of some among them; and you are one of those, my dear—you are one of those.'

He paused for a little while, and then took her unresisting hand and laid it on his breast.

'I had a strange yearning to see you once more, Mary; a fancy that grew stronger as my health declined. I thought I could safely venture without chance of recognition, I was so much changed—so many old acquaintances had failed to remember me when they met me in the street. I am such a mere wreck of what I once was, and I so longed to see you again, my dear; for I never loved any woman as I loved you, though I was base enough to be tempted away from you by Esther Greenock's money. I had my reward. O Mary, you could never imagine the life I led with that woman. It was one perpetual scene of ill-temper and repining. I had sold myself into bondage for a pittance. I felt myself the meanest and most degraded of mankind. My life has been one long series of failures; and I come to you at last, a poor broken-down creature, to seek comfort from the dear soul I wronged so basely.'

'Do not speak of that—do not remember it now. Our lives are gone; they might have been different.

Yes, James, I think we might have been happy together. I am very glad you came back to me. It has been sweet to me to nurse and watch you all through this weary illness.'

'And I have only come back to be a burden upon you at the last! That seems hard, Mary.'

'Nothing could be so hard to me as not to see you again. In all these years that have gone by, there has never been a day in which I have not thought of you and prayed for you.'

'You ought to have hated or despised me, Mary.'

'I have never changed in my love for you,' she answered gently.

He lifted her hand to his lips, and held it there till he fell asleep, she still kneeling by his side.

When he awoke by and by, his senses were wandering a little. He talked of the mill, and the trout-stream by which they had walked together so often, almost as if he fancied himself a young man again. The doctor shook his head gravely when he came in, late in the evening, to look at his patient, and told Mary that the end was very near.

The end came at daybreak next morning.

To the last James Herriston's dim eyes sought the face he had once loved; to the last, amid all the wandering of his thoughts, the feeble hand clasped that other hand. His head lay on Mary Baxter's breast when he died, looking up at her till the very end; and his latest breath murmured her name.

This was her reward for thirty years' constancy. She bore his death with a strange calmness, and it was she who ordered the simple arrangements of the funeral, for which the two sisters would have to pay out of their slender means. She showed her sister the name upon their lodger's coffin with a faint sad smile.

'You did not remember him, did you, Harriet?'

'No indeed, Mary. I never knew any one so changed.'

'Not to me, my dear; he never changed to me. I have loved him all my life.'

PRINTED BY TROWITZSCH & SON, BERLIN.